D0679989

HANG 'EM ALL

HANG 'EM ALL

by

David Whitehead

Dales Large Print Books
Long Preston, North Yorkshire,
BD23 4ND, England.

British Library Cataloguing in Publication Data.

Whitehead, David
    Hang 'em all.

    A catalogue record of this book is
    available from the British Library

    ISBN   978-1-84262-776-1 pbk

First published in Great Britain in 1989 by Robert Hale Limited

Copyright © David Whitehead 1989

Cover illustration © Gordon Crabb by arrangement with
Alison Eldred

Published in Large Print 2010 by arrangement with
David Whitehead

Dales Large Print is an imprint of Library Magna Books Ltd.

Printed and bound in Great Britain by
T.J. (International) Ltd., Cornwall, PL28 8RW

Dedicated to the memory of
Pat Shelley,
a good man dearly loved
and sorely missed.

ONE

There are times when a man can almost *smell* trouble coming.

Town Marshal Sam Judge could.

He smelled it now.

One minute he'd been dozing in the chair outside the law office with his stovepipes up on the hitch-rack, letting the pre-dawn chill chase the last sleepy cobwebs from his mind; the next he'd tensed almost imperceptibly and slit his calm grey eyes to scan his immediate surroundings.

He saw nothing, no other signs of life anywhere.

Yet.

Five minutes later he heard the sound of horses' hooves in the distance. Two minutes after that six riders appeared at the end of First Street.

Sam didn't move a muscle but stayed exactly where he was, watching them from beneath his hat-brim, to all intents and purposes still asleep.

He couldn't make out many details at first, because they were coming in from the east and they had the sun, just climbing above the jagged Sangre de Christos ten or fifteen miles away, behind them. But he saw that they were fanned out, riding stirrup to stirrup, and coming on at a walk.

He watched them ride closer.

Their horses, he saw, were a mixture of duns and bays and paints, none of them in particularly good condition, and the men riding them looked just as back-bent and weary. Four of them were white, one a Mexican, the sixth a black feller. They favoured standard range gear – levis, check shirts, vests. The Mex wore a fancy pair of woolly chaps, the negro a heavy broadcloth jacket. All of them wore guns.

Their hats were broad-brimmed and pulled low. One of them sported rust-coloured whiskers and tight black gloves. Another wore two guns in a finely-tooled *buscadero* weapons belt. One man the marshal noticed in particular because of the sharp-rowelled Spanish colonial spurs on his high-heeled boots, and the puffed scars they'd left on his bay's underbelly.

Not one of them was older than twenty-five summers, he decided. But now that they were abreast of him, he saw the old men's eyes in their otherwise youthful faces and knew that each of them had likely seen more bloodshed than many a man twice their age.

Curiously, he found himself pitying them.

Then they'd ridden past.

Sam followed them with his eyes, not moving his head lest they tumble to the fact that he'd been watching them all along. They reined in about two hundred feet down the street, cooled their saddles at the corner of First and Porter and tied their animals to the hitch-rack outside Katy Larrimer's greasy spoon cafe.

Sitting as still as a statue, the marshal

heard the clatter their boots made on the boardwalk; one of them say something; another one laugh. Then the bell above Katy's door jangled and the door itself closed behind them.

After that – silence.

That early, First Street was still empty. In another half-hour the stores'd open up and Austin Springs would get just as busy as it did every other day save Sundays and Christmas.

Right then, though, the town was still quiet enough for Sam to hear the Rio Grande chuckling by a quarter of a mile outside the town limits and listen to a flock of wild geese crossing the cloud-free sky like a living arrowhead.

Quiet enough to sit and wonder about the six hellions who'd just ridden in.

'Course, he didn't know for a *fact* that they were firebrands. They weren't exactly wearing signs. But as a veteran peace officer, Sam guessed he'd spent enough years locking horns with similar types to believe he'd correctly read *this* little crew for what it was.

The sun climbed higher, faster, melting the shadows still stuck in doorways and alleys and such. It looked like it was going to be another hot one, he decided, getting up to stretch and yawn. But that was no surprise; the days were nearly always hot in that part of southern Colorado around the middle of June.

Checking the street one final time, he disappeared into the square, solidly-built adobe structure behind him.

He was a tall man, about six feet two or three, raw-boned and hard-muscled, with a lean, weather-beaten face, gentle grey eyes and a narrow, lipless mouth. The hair beneath his round-crowned buff-coloured Stetson was black shot through with grey, and thinning. The little finger of his right hand was missing. And up around the eyes and nose he had the look of a one-time pugilist who'd never quite been able to dodge all the blows.

He was in no way a thing of beauty. At

forty-five years of age, he was still the same moody and often impatient man he'd always been. But likewise, folks who knew him well also knew that he had a tender, even sensitive side, and could – when he chose to – share a joke with the best of them.

With a sigh he flopped into the creaky swivel chair behind his old mahogany desk and pulled a cigar from the humidor in front of him. Looking at it, he shook his head. In the old days, when his reputation as a town-tamer had made him a minor celebrity, he'd smoked dollar cigars one in each hand. But now he was down to these noxious three-for-a-dime weeds from Yale's Emporium on Cameron Street.

Still, a cigar was a cigar, or so he kept telling himself as he bit off the end, spat it into a nearby cuspidor and got it working with a match he scratched along the edge of the desk.

Soon he was viewing the cluttered, dark-panelled office through a haze of blue smoke.

It had been a quiet week in the Springs. Hell, if he was going to be honest about it, it had been a quiet *year*. And as usual, he had that big old place all to himself and he wasn't much enjoying it.

The room was full of memories, from the dusty, now rarely-used rifle-rack to four chipped enamel mugs hanging forgotten on wall-pegs above the stove. But it hadn't always been like that. Time was when those four cells out back had been fit to bust with all the trouble-makers he'd run into 'em.

'Course, that was back in '72, when the Springs had been as wild as wild could be. He'd had three full-time deputies then, and needed 'em, too.

But now...

Maybe all that talk he'd been hearing was true. Maybe the west *had* been tamed for good and all. It sure seemed hard to believe now that the Springs had ever been a hell-town, because these days it might just as well have been a cemetery for all the living that got done in it.

Ah, but seven, eight years ago... He blew a smoke ring as warmth flickered into his eyes. Now those *were* the days. You didn't dare go patrolling the streets back then without you cradled a ten-gauge in your arms, for there was a murder a week on average, often more.

In fact, Austin Springs had been so lawless that the town council had tried to hire Bill Hickok to come in and clean it up, on account of what he'd already done as city marshal of Abilene. But old Jimmy, as Sam had always known him, had had too good a thing going for him over in Kansas to bother with a rowdy Colorado hell-town – by which he'd meant a hundred and fifty dollars a month plus a percentage of whatever fines he was able to collect.

Sam now, he hadn't been so picky. The order had been tall but the deal had been fair. So he'd pinned on their badge and tamed their town, just the way he'd tamed a score like it over the years.

Only trouble was, instead of moving on

when the job was finished, he'd stuck around, and thinking back on it, that had been his single biggest mistake; allowing himself to grow *old* here, old and soft...

Suddenly a coughing fit seized him and he sat forward, spluttering. Damned cigars, he thought, as he struggled for breath. Maybe he ought to consider cutting down or changing brands.

As breathing became damn' nigh impossible, he went very red in the face. He choked up, rearranging the phlegm inside his chest, drew in one breath, another. Gradually his lungs loosened up. By the time he had fully recovered, a fat Abyssinian cat with mottled tan-white fur and expressive sea-green eyes had hopped up onto the desk to study him intently.

Mitzi – he'd named her after a whore he'd once known in Black Rock, Nevada – had wandered into his office one day about three years earlier and promptly adopted him. Nobody knew where she'd come from, or why she'd picked him. But pick him she had.

She peered into his face with her head cocked to one side.

''S'all right, Mitz,' the marshal said, clearing his throat one final time. 'You can wipe that worried look off your face now. I think I'll survive.'

Reassured by his tone, the cat came forward to flop heavily into his lap, where she quickly twisted over onto her back so that he could scratch at her belly.

'Talking to cats now, Sam?'

The lawman looked up as Jack O'Neal, the mayor of Austin Springs, came through the door. 'Sometimes they're the only ones that'll listen,' he replied easily.

O'Neal, a smartly-dressed Irishman with a smooth, tanned skin and snow-white hair, frowned. He looked much younger than his fifty years, and his clear blue eyes were sharp and vital. 'That sounds ominous,' he said, coming to stand before the desk. 'You got problems, Sam?'

'Oh, nothin' that a decent cigar couldn't settle,' the marshal replied, smiling. ''Mornin', Jack. Pull up a chair. How's tricks?'

'Fine, fine.' As he spoke, O'Neal reached into his tailored grey Prince Albert and brought out a thin cardboard tube which he tossed to the lawman. Sam knew from many years' experience that the tube contained an expensive, hand-rolled Havana, and nodded his thanks. 'I just thought I'd call by to remind you about–'

'No need,' Sam cut in. 'If it's about Redmond, I'm going out to his place today. Right after I get me a shave and some breakfast, in fact.'

'Good,' the mayor replied. Standing there in the gradually-lightening office, he looked the picture of sophistication. Once a prominent west coast businessman, he had come out from San Francisco about three years before and invested heavily in a number of local enterprises, from Austin Springs' bi-weekly newspaper to a half-ownership in the Saddle of Faith Saloon over on Mitchell Street. He was a decent enough sort, considering he was a man with political ambitions, and Sam got along well with him. 'Collecting taxes for the U.S. Land Office is an important chore, Sam, and as you know, Redmond's well overdue.'

'Well, I'd hardly call bein' a week late *that*,' the marshal said mildly. 'Don't forget, that spread of his is fifteen, twenty miles from here, Jack, and he's had to run it all by hisself ever since his wife got pregnant. Ain't always easy to get into town on time.'

'Maybe. But–'

Further comment was cancelled as a gunshot ripped through the early-morning silence, followed closely by a woman's scream.

'What the devil was that?' gasped the mayor, spinning around.

Sam didn't waste time telling him. Even before the question was fully voiced he was up, the cat falling from his lap with a surprised meow, and out the door.

He reached the boardwalk just as the shot's last echo was replaced by the distant barking of excited dogs. Stepping down into the dirt, he glanced up and down the street. Nearby, a rider was trying to calm his skittish mount. Further along, a farmer had stalled his heavy wagon and was peering around, clearly puzzled. Folks afoot had appeared at doors and windows, or stopped in mid-stride to find out what in hell was going on.

Ignoring them all, Sam hurried toward Katy Larrimer's cafe, thumbing the leather thong off the hammer of his Remington Army .44 in case he should need to get to it fast.

Heck Mabey appeared in his path. The big bald butcher was still clutching a long-bladed knife in his right fist. 'What's goin' on, Sam?' he asked anxiously.

Sam shook his head. 'Not now, Heck, I ain't got the time.'

He made it to the corner of First and Porter and went straight up onto the opposite boardwalk into the cafe. The jangling of the bell over the door sounded unnaturally loud in the sudden silence.

The eaterie was large and brick-built. As he entered, it looked bright and clean and normal. Five of the six young men who'd ridden into town twenty minutes earlier were sitting at a centre table. The one on his feet – the one who favoured the two-gun *buscadero* rig – was still holding his left-side Tranter and sharing some private joke with his cronies. They were the only customers.

Katy Larrimer was standing in the arched doorway leading back into the kitchen, pale and trembling. One small, work-roughened hand was pressed tight to her mouth.

All eyes turned to Sam as he scanned the room, his gaze finally dropping to the knee-high bullet hole in the wall beside the door.

''Mornin', marshal,' said the man with the red hair and tight black gloves. 'Come to tie on the nosebag, have you?'

The others laughed, all but the one standing up, who went very pale.

Ignoring them, Sam fired his quiet, calm question at the tearful woman. 'What happened, Kate?'

The matronly widow shook her greying head slowly, as if coming out of a dream, and her blue eyes focused on him only with effort. She was short and stout, wearing a too-tight checked dress, and her sixty-year-old face was bloodless and spectral.

'I–'

'I'll tell you what happened, marshal,' said the red-head, who appeared to be their leader.

Sam shot him a brief glance. 'I didn't ask you,' he replied. 'Katy?'

She sniffed, cleared her throat. 'They … they came in. I t … took their order. Bacon, rolls…' She shook her head again. 'I went out back to start it cookin'–'

'Yeah,' said Red. 'And while we're waitin', Matt here spots a goddamn cockroach crawlin' up the wall. A big, fat, ugly-lookin' *cockroach.*'

Slowly Sam turned his gaze to the table at which the newcomers were seated. The red-head, he saw, was about twenty-four or so, with a pasty, oval face and freckles splashed like rust-spots across his snub nose.

'So bein' the big brave boys that you are,' he replied sarcastically, 'you thought you'd use it for target practice, huh?'

The feller called Matt found his voice at last. 'Let's just say that I don't take kindly to eatin' in a place that's got bugs crawlin' up the walls,' he said quietly.

Sam focused on him then, saw something vaguely familiar about his long, moody face and tall, slim build, and was just about to dismiss it when he realised exactly which 'Matt' this was.

It was Matt Dury.

His son.

It was a long, long story. Too long to go into now. So the marshal just cleared his throat, swallowed hard and said, 'Put that gun away, Matt.'

Red, seated beside the young man in the two-gun rig, threw a quick, puzzled glance from one of them to the other. There was no doubt that the marshal had been badly shaken by the unexpected encounter. Matt's reaction, however, was more difficult to cipher. 'You *know* this lawdog?' he asked.

Without taking his eyes off Sam, Matt nodded. 'Yep,' he said softly. 'I know him.' He slipped the Tranter back into leather, then held his hands away from his sides. 'Better?' he asked amiably.

'Better,' said the marshal. 'Now get on over here.'

'Huh?'

'You heard me,' Sam snapped quickly. 'You're under arrest.'

Matt looked blank. 'Under–? What's the charge?'

'Disturbin' the peace.'

The young Mexican member of the group, who'd been seated at the head of the table, chose that moment to climb to his feet, his dark-skinned hands brushing imaginary dust off the gunbelt strapped around his narrow hips. 'S'all right, Matt,' he said with almost comical Spanish formality. 'I'll take care of this.' To Sam he said, 'Back off, lawman. Leave us be. We don't want no trouble – and neither do you.'

Giving no sign that he'd heard the Mexican, Sam said, 'Time's a-wastin', Matt. You comin' quietly, or what?'

Before Matt could reply, the Mexican pushed his chair back noisily and let his clawed right hand hover above the grips of his Peacemaker. He looked ridiculous in his woolly chaps and wide-brimmed sombrero, a boy trying hard to be a man. He was about twenty-two, twenty-three, with a dark, pocked skin and the beginnings of a narrow moustache draped along his upper lip. His black eyes, however, were hooded and dangerous. They alone were enough to make sure Sam took him seriously.

'Back off, lawman,' he repeated through clenched teeth. 'Do it, or else.'

His friends were watching Sam closely now, wondering which way he was going to jump. Sam, however, only looked down at the Mexican and smiled.

'I mean it, old-timer!' the boy hissed,

showing his white teeth in a snarl.

It was very quiet in the cafe. For one split second Sam's eyes dropped to the Mexican's gun hand. He saw it tremble. The crazy kid was just liable to try it, he realised. Almost imperceptibly he shifted his weight, deciding coolly on a shoulder-shot, a crippling wound, not a killing one.

Then–

'Forget it, Raul.' It was Matt.

'*Que?*' The Mexican blinked sweat out of his eyes.

'I said forget it. If he wants to take me in, let him. It's not worth gettin' killed over.'

The Mexican frowned. 'Killed?' He swore in Spanish. 'You got a lot of faith in me, don't you?'

A brief smile crossed Matt's face. 'You ought to be thankin' me, *amigo*. I'm savin' your skinny little hide, 'cause unless this "old-timer's" slowed up any – which I doubt – he'd have you plugged and on your way to hell before you could even *touch* iron, let alone pull it.' He eyed the marshal. 'That right, Sam?'

Sam inclined his head. 'That's right,' he replied. As the youngster came over to join him at the door, the marshal turned to Katy. 'Soon as I lock this here miscreant up, I'll be back for breakfast. Two over-easies, some bacon and a small stack of pancakes. Got that?'

The widow nodded. 'S ... sure.'

'Shouldn't be no more'n about ten, fifteen minutes,' he went on, eyeing Red, Raul and their friends. 'So you fellers got that long to cough up five dollars damages for the lady here and get the hell outta my town.'

'Hey, now listen here—'

'Was I you, I'd shut it, Red,' Sam cut in, his tone leaving no room for argument.

Red did.

With one last withering look at the five young hardcases, the marshal turned, and together he and Matt stepped out onto the street.

They didn't speak again until they were

halfway back to the law office.

'Well, I sure never expected to see you again,' Sam said awkwardly, still trying to mask his shaken nerves.

'Same here,' the young man beside him replied. He didn't know that Sam was his real father, only that he had been a family friend back in the old days and a man he used to call uncle, so conversation came that much easier to him. 'We heard about you for a while, ma and me. Bought into a joy-house on the Barbary Coast, didn't you?'

Sam smiled at the memory. Now that the tension had passed, First Street had returned to normal, and they had to dodge wagons and horseback riders fast in order to make it across the street in one piece. 'Yep,' he replied. 'Back in '70, '71. But I only stuck it for six months. It was a good life. Easy, too. But somehow I never cared much for it.'

'So you went back to star-packin',' Matt said, shaking his head. 'Know somethin', Sam? It's good to see you. It really is. Truth to tell, I thought you was dead. Figured you must'a stopped a bullet with your head *years* ago.'

The marshal summoned a hollow chuckle. 'Not hardly,' he replied, eyeing his companion covertly.

Matt had grown straight and tall since those early days, when he had been a lardy, mischievous child. The face was long, lived-in and weathered by the elements, yet still somehow innocent. His eyes were darker than Sam's, more the colour of gunmetal, his features shaped more by his mother, who had been a handsome woman to say the least. His hair was short, black and curly, his chin square, rugged, and pitted by a dimple. He wore low boots, striped California pants and a plain nankeen shirt beneath a worn leather vest, and cut such a fine figure striding along the boardwalk that Sam had to fight down the sudden rush of pride that brought a lump to his throat.

At last they reached the dark, still-cool law office, where Jack O'Neal was waiting anxiously inside the doorway. Seeing the lawman, he relaxed visibly.

'Sam! What in tarnation—'

'S'all right, Jack,' the marshal cut in, pushing past him and taking off his hat. 'No need to get your bowels in an uproar.'

'But that shot – the scream—'

'Just a couple of young fellers feelin' rumbustious, that's all.'

'No trouble then?' the mayor asked keenly.

'Not so's you'd notice. They're fittin'ly sheepish and willin' to pay fer damages, so it's all over and done with.'

Satisfied, Jack's blue eyes lit on Matt. 'Who's your friend?' he asked, following them back into the office.

Sam glanced at his companion, fighting hard to keep his voice even. 'This is, ah, my nephew, Matt Dury, from out of Brown-wood, Texas. Matt, meet Jack O'Neal, the mayor of Austin Springs.' To Jack he explained, 'Me an' Matt ain't seen each other in fifteen years or more. He just got in.'

Matt and the mayor shook hands and ex-changed pleasantries. Then, being an industrious sort, O'Neal excused himself, saying, 'You two must have a lot of catching up to do, so I'll leave you to it. But don't forget Redmond, Sam.'

'As if I could.'

After Jack left them, Sam and his son were left alone in the office. Even Mitzi had wandered off someplace else. Sam struggled valiantly to find something to say, but all he could come up with was, 'Grab a chair, boy. Take the weight off. Coffee?'

Matt glanced at the pot on the stove. 'Thanks.'

Sam went over and took down two mugs, blowing in each to shift the dust. He poured coffee, turned back and held out a cup. As Matt took it, the marshal said quietly, 'That was a damn' fool thing you did just now. Shootin' at bugs.'

But Matt only chuckled. 'Well, sometimes you gotta make allowances, Sam. We been on the trail ever since Duquesne, see. Which, in case you didn't know it, is quite a ways to come without lettin' off a little steam.'

'I guess. Duquesne? That where you boys hail from?'

'Hell no. All over. But Duquesne was the last burg we stayed in for any length o' time.'

Sam sat down on the edge of his desk. 'What brings you to Austin Springs?' he asked casually.

Evading his gaze, Matt glanced out the window, listening to the sounds of the town busying up. 'Oh, this 'n' that. You know. Re-supplyin', mostly.'

Sam nodded. 'I ask because they look a rough crew, them friends o' yourn.' His face was obscured by the steam rising from his cup. 'Wouldn't want to think of you mixin' in with the wrong sort,' he said pointedly.

Matt looked back at him. 'I *am* the wrong sort,' he said in the kind of tone that made it hard for Sam to tell whether or not he was joshing. 'They, ah, they keep you busy around here?'

'Oh, so-so.'

'Look after you?'

'Sure. Eighty a month an' found. Free

meals. Nice little room over on Cameron Street.' He nodded, almost trying to convince himself. 'It does for me.'

He took another swallow of coffee, then asked the question that had been uppermost in his mind ever since he'd first clapped eyes on Matt again. 'How's your ma these days? Still livin' in Brownwood?'

Matt glanced down at the mug in his hands. 'Well, she's still there,' he replied quietly. 'But she ain't livin' no more. Died about half a year back, Sam. The pneumonia.'

Something died inside Sam too, when he heard that, because back when the whole world'd seemed younger, he'd been mighty smitten by Matt's mother, and she'd been similarly attracted to him, too. Might even have grown serious enough to wed – if she hadn't already been married to Bob Dury, Sam's closest friend and fellow Texas Ranger.

To this day he still felt guilty about what had happened between him and Rosie that fine October afternoon, with Bob off on a routine patrol of the Brazos. Guilty because what they'd done was wrong, rash and downright *stupid*.

Still, at least Bob never found out. Right up until a Minie ball scrambled his guts at the top of Cemetery Ridge back in '63, he'd been just as proud of 'his' son as any real father could be. That Matt was really Sam's progeny had remained their secret, his and Rosie's. And now … now it was just his.

'I'm right sorry to hear that,' the marshal muttered sincerely. 'She was a fine woman, Matt.'

Matt nodded moodily. 'That she was,' he agreed with a sigh. 'Well, I guess you'll be wantin' my guns now, huh?'

Sam forced a smile. 'Guess again.'

'Huh?'

'Go on, get outta here,' he growled good-naturedly. 'I must be gettin' soft in the brain, lettin' such a mean *hombre* go free, but what the hell? We're family, ain't we? Practically?'

As the marshal and his boy traded stares,

Sam saw the same painful, young-old look on Matt's face that he'd seen on those of his comrades. One minute he was the kid Sam had known back home in Texas, the next he was a stranger; worse, a *dangerous* stranger.

'Thanks, *amigo*,' Matt nodded, standing up. 'I 'preciate it.'

Feeling his spirits lift, Sam shrugged. 'Forget it. But what say we get together again tonight. I gotta ride out to a ranch on the other side of Tom Smith Creek in a while, but I'll be back by five, six o'clock. We could have supper, chew the fat over old times.'

Matt's gunmetal eyes softened a little. 'I'd like that, Sam. But you told us to get out of town, remember?'

The lawman shook his head. 'I told *them* to get out of town,' he corrected.

A dour smile crossed Matt's face. 'I *am* them,' he said. 'Where they go, I go.'

The lawman shrugged again. 'I'm sorry to hear that, boy. Feller like you should have better friends. *Real* friends.'

Matt nodded. 'Daresay you're right. But

until real friends come along...' He let the sentence hang.

Sam swallowed. There was plenty he wanted to say, but he stopped himself. A man had to make his own way through life, learn from his own mistakes. And that's what Matt was now – a man.

Anyway, he thought sourly, *it's a bit late to start acting all paternal dammit.*

He extended his hand. 'Well, good luck to you,' he said gently.

Matt took the hand. They shook. *'Vaya con Dios,'* he replied, turning away quickly. At the door, however, he swung back. 'Sam?'

The marshal looked up from his paper-work, eyes narrowed. 'Yeah?'

For one brief second he thought he saw a struggle of sorts taking place on the boy's face, as if he were trying to make an important decision. Then it was gone – if it had ever really been there. Maybe it had only been a trick of the light. 'Nothin',' Matt said, forcing a smile. 'So long, *amigo.*'

Sam listened to his heavy, confident

strides until they were lost in the distance. Only then did he mutter, 'So long,' to the empty office.

TWO

By the time Sam got back over to Katy Larrimer's eaterie, there was no sign of Matt's five 'friends', nor of Matt himself. But Katy sure looked better, he noticed, as he watched her hurry back and forth between tables, taking and delivering orders in her usual business-like way.

The place had crowded up some since Sam's earlier visit, but his order of two over-easies, some bacon and a stack of pancakes arrived almost as soon as he found himself a table. Furthermore, everything he'd asked for had been doubled, and a few extras – grits, tomatoes and pinto beans – added for good measure.

'Compliments of the management,' Katy explained with a wink.

He winked back. 'Obliged,' he nodded. 'Them boys pay up all right, by the way?'

Her grey head dipped once, sharply. 'Five dollars, just like you told 'em,' she replied. 'Thanks, Sam. I guess it's been so long since anyone fired a gun in Austin Springs that I just went to pieces.'

Left alone, he set about his breakfast, but moodily and with little real appetite. His chance encounter with Matt Dury had stirred up a hornet's nest of half-buried memories and now he felt restless, more restless than he'd been in many a month.

It just didn't sit right with him to let a decent young feller like Matt waste his life riding – and siding – with that pack of trail wolves. They were grief, the lot of them, and Lord alone knew what trouble they'd wind up getting his boy into.

Perhaps he should've done more. Spelled it out to Matt when he'd had the chance. Warned him away from 'em. But ... hell, as he'd told himself back at the office, it was a little late to start facing up to his responsibilities now – and maybe that was why he felt so lousy.

He washed the food down with good hot coffee, black as sin and sweet as syrup, just how he liked it, then stopped by the barber shop on Porter to get a shave. After that, he marched on up to the Erdoes Street Livery to collect his horse in preparation for the ride out to John Redmond's ranch.

Around him Austin Springs was a riot of activity, and not at all the same sleepy little town it had been at dawn. Farmers were driving high-sided wagons laden with wheat, beans, maize and spuds to market. A team of freighters were loading some heavy machinery aboard two waiting Studebakers, readying it for delivery to one of the tin or copper mines studding the foothills about twelve miles to the east.

Shoppers crowded the busy sidewalks; children played noisily over at the elementary school; the Colorado State Bank was doing good business and as he walked, Sam heard the 8.30 Denver, South Park & Pacific northbound roll into the rail depot with a shrill greeting whistle.

Yesiree, he told himself again. Austin Springs is tame now. Civilised.

But curiously, that thought only added to his depression.

Sam's horse turned out to be a pretty smart old strawberry roan called Charlie. Just seeing the creature raised Sam's flagging spirits. He ran one calloused hand across its pronounced red coat, checking its back for sores and its legs for scratches or infirmities, and finding none, saddled up.

Soon the town lay behind them, and Sam headed north across the flatlands towards Tom Smith Creek and beyond.

Around him the land rose and fell like wrinkles in a blanket. Thick blue grama muffled the sound of his horse's hooves. The sun threw his shadow off to the left. For a while he watched it skitter along beside him,

41

his only companion. Away to the east, the Sangre de Christos rose purple against blue, shimmering across the fifteen-mile distance, one minute light, the next minute dark with the passage of slow-moving clouds across the sun.

For a while he was able to forget the town and his problems, and just lose himself in the monotonous tattoo of his horse's pounding hooves and the constant flow of up-down grassland unfolding like a tread-mill beneath him.

After a couple of hours he came to the creek, a shallow but fast-running stream that could be traced in one form or another all the way back to the Arkansas River seventy or eighty miles further north. By that time it was heading towards eleven o'clock and growing steadily warmer, so man and horse took a well-earned breather before continuing their journey.

Flies zipped through the air, joining the bees and butterflies clustered around patches of colourful wild flowers – Indian paint-

brush, rosecrown and red and blue columbine. Timber sprang up, Engelmann spruce
and golden aspen. The trees stood tall, proud
and impassive. Passing through them some
time later was like passing through a different
world where everything was cool, shady and
muted. Beyond the trees the land flattened
out, greened-up even more, rose gradually.
And then–

At the crest of the ridge Sam reined in to
look down at John Redmond's modest little
ranch.

It wasn't much – the main house, a high-
roofed barn, stable and corral, all built from
rough-hewn timber. Two dogs fought over
scraps in the front yard. A couple of
chickens clucked and strutted. But oddly,
they were the only signs of life.

Frowning, Sam kicked the roan into
motion, descending the gentle incline slowly
and with caution. For the first time in four
hours he spoke.

'Hello the house!'

But there was no reply.

He rode nearer, calling out again as he walked the roan into the yard, scattering the chickens.

Ten seconds passed more like ten minutes. The dogs ran off, barking playfully. Sam leaned forward with a creak of saddle leather, trying to see beyond the blindness of the closed windows. Over in the stable a horse stamped its hooves.

He didn't like it. Didn't like it at all.

But before he could do anything about it–

The scratching of poorly-tended hinges carried to him on the faint mid-day breeze. The door of the shack – for really it was little more than that – was opening slowly.

Expecting trouble, Sam let his right hand fall to the butt of his Remington, but before he could reach it–

Nell Redmond stepped out onto the gloomy porch, her distended stomach stretching the fabric of her flowery dress. She was twenty-six but looked older, of well-to-do Minnesota stock but now just as poor as poor could be. Her face was pale, pretty gone bad, her hair, save for one long strand hanging down across her high forehead, pulled back almost painfully into a bun. She frowned. Her dark, tired eyes squinted. She said one word.

'Marshal?'

He cleared his throat. 'Afternoon, Mrs Redmond. Is your husband around?'

She came forward into the sunlight, ungainly in her pregnancy. 'Oh, marshal! Thank God!'

Noting the dangerous way she swayed back and forth, he swung down from the saddle without waiting to be invited, and leaving Charlie ground-hitched, hurried across to grab her before she fell and hurt herself.

Holding her by the elbows, he waited until she regained control of herself before asking her what was wrong.

'John,' she said, indicating the shack. Her eyes still lacked focus, but now she seemed strong enough to stand unaided. 'Had an accident,' she muttered.

'He's inside?' Sam asked sharply.

She nodded. 'Sleep now. But hurtin', marshal. Hurtin' bad.'

He went into the shack and pulled up sharp. The single room was dark, full of stale air, a mess. He wanted to pull the drapes, open the windows, clear all the clutter to one side, but knew that his first responsibility lay with the wounded man. He glanced around the room, almost missed the cot at first, then crossed to it, double-quick.

John Redmond was of a similar age to his wife. He was a good-looking man with a curly mop of black hair; tall, barrel-chested, thick in the arms. He was stretched out on his back, covered with a blanket, eyes shut, and so pale that his skin seemed to glow through the gloom. Sam knelt beside him, gave him a brief examination, then turned to find Nell framed worriedly in the doorway.

'What happened?' he asked quietly.

She came a step nearer, shrugged, clutched at her stomach as if to ease it. 'Las' Tuesday it was,' she replied. 'He was outside, breakin' one o' them mustangs he brought down from the high country last month.' She stared over his shoulder, at her husband. 'Somethin' happened, I don't know what. The two of 'em fell, the horse rolled over him. He said his stomach was on fire...'

Her little-girl-lost voice trailed away.

'You managed to get him into the house?' he guessed. 'Onto the bed?'

She nodded. 'Had to,' she replied. 'He couldn't move for himself, marshal.' Her eyes came up to rake his face. 'Will he be all right? He ain't been able to take food nor drink ever since it happened. All he does is lay there an' sleep.'

Sam shrugged. What could he tell her? He turned back to the man on the cot and gently pulled back the blanket. Redmond didn't even stir. As carefully as he could, the marshal unbuttoned the horse-rancher's shirt and pulled it open to reveal a chest almost black with bruises.

'He coughed up any blood, do you know?' he asked the woman without looking around.

Nell came closer. 'No sir. That's good though, ain't it?'

He nodded, reaching forward to peel back Redmond's eyelids. The eyes were glazed, unseeing. 'Pull back that curtain, will you? Let's have some light 'n' air in here.'

Behind him, Nell did as she was told. Finally Sam got back to his feet.

'Well?' she asked, clearly dreading the answer.

He looked her straight in the eye. 'I'm no doctor,' he replied. 'But to me it looks just about as bad as it can get without bein' fatal. He's practically broke every rib in him, an' maybe his back as well.'

She sagged again.

Redmond's eyes had told him something else; one pupil was wider than the other, a sure sign of internal bleeding. But he didn't mention that to the woman – she was in enough of a state at it was.

'Oh, my poor Johnny–'

'Now, now, Mrs Redmond. I know it's hard, but you gotta be strong. Long as your man's still breathin', he's got a chance, right?'

She nodded. 'I guess. But–'

'Just stay here an' keep him wrapped up warm while I hightail it back to town an' fetch Doc Hobson.'

'Would you?' She grabbed his arm, her display of gratitude pitiful. 'Oh, God bless you, marshal...'

Somehow he disengaged himself from her and went back outside. It had taken him four hours to get here. If he pushed it, he could possibly get back to town in about three. But rush as he might, there was no way the county's only doctor was going to get back here in less than seven hours. *Damn.*

Still, John Redmond had lasted this long. If he could just hang on a while longer...

Sam swung aboard Charlie and offered the woman a brief salute. There was nothing more to say, so he urged the roan to speed and left the front yard at a gallop, heading back up and over the ridge, retracing his route to civilisation.

There were some days, he told himself thirty sore-assed minutes later, when a feller shouldn't oughta get out of bed.

'And this is one of 'em,' he muttered to the heaving horse beneath him.

He didn't dream that his day was just about to get worse.

He was too busy worrying about his horse, for one thing. How much hard riding could he take? Charlie wasn't as young nor as spry as he used to be – hell, Sam neither, for that matter. But still he pushed them both to the limit.

The old roan fairly flew across a sea of wind-rippled grass, back through the cool timber, up slopes, down into flower-littered valleys, uncomplaining and apparently tireless. But by the time they reached Tom Smith Creek again, man and horse were both breathing hard.

Sam reined in reluctantly, but knowing it was the sensible thing to do. As much as he wanted to get the medic out to Redmond, there was little point in running his horse into the ground and having to make the rest of the journey on foot.

So he waited until Charlie's ragged breathing had settled down some, then allowed him to drink from the creek.

'Good feller ... good feller... That's enough now, don't want you too loggy to ride...'

Sam took off his hat and ran a forearm across his red forehead. He was sweating like a pig. *Gettin' too old for all this gallivantin', I guess.*

He reached for his canteen, uncapped it and took a pull, working the water around his mouth before spitting. He swallowed the next swig; the water was warm but came welcome all the same. Bending, he refilled the canteen, then tied it around his pommel.

'All right, boy. Let's get movin'.'

He was just about to remount when he heard a distant drum-roll of hooves coming his way at speed. Pausing with one foot in the stirrup, he narrowed his eyes and scanned the surrounding area.

He spotted the rider almost immediately. He was coming in from the south – whoever *he* was – and pushing his horse as if he had a demon on his tail.

Sam left Charlie where he was and moved off about ten feet to get a better look at the newcomer. He was immediately on the alert; after all, the rider was coming out from the direction of town.

When he was about two hundred feet away, Sam identified him with a muttered – and mystified – 'Heck?' For it was just about the last person the tall lawman expected to see riding across the desolate plains – Heck Mabey, one of Austin Springs' two butchers.

Sam raised his hat and waved it high to attract the other man's attention. When the butcher saw him, he turned his horse towards him, splashing recklessly through the creek's shallow bed and hauling back on the reins at the last minute to bring his lathery paint to a grass-shredding halt.

'Sam! Thought I was never gonna find yuh!'

Sam frowned, trying unsuccessfully to shake off the feeling of dread in his stomach. 'What's wrong, Heck? What's happened?'

Heck practically fell out of his saddle. He looked even more beat than Sam and Charlie put together – but that was probably because he wasn't used to hard riding.

A great big bear of a man with a bald head and a black walrus moustache, he raised much of his own stock on the modest little spread he and his wife owned up around Blanca Peak. Many's the time Sam had watched him working away at his block, using knife and cleaver with a skill that most Comanche would sell their favourite squaws to possess. But although the stink of blood and the squealing of throat-slit pigs had no obvious effect on him, he was a man who scared easy, and often.

Like now.

'Heck, I ast you a question!' Sam prodded impatiently.

The butcher nodded, gasping to get his breath back. He kneaded the reins in his big hands with much agitation. 'Oh Lord, it's terrible, Sam! Jack O'Neal sent me out to find you, said you'd be out to Redmond's place, but I took the wrong trail and–'

'*What's happened, dammit!*'

The savagery with which Sam asked the question cut through Heck's blue funk. Abruptly he stiffened, looking even paler than usual. 'They robbed the bank, Sam!'

Sam asked the question even though he already knew the answer. 'Who?'

'Them fellers as rode in this mornin'. Jack said–'

But Sam wasn't listening. His mind was still reeling from this new turn of events. The Colorado State Bank robbed? By – ah, God, no… He sagged, suddenly tired beyond his years. By Matt and his five friends?

'When?'

Heck shook his head, flustered. 'Around eleven o'clock.'

'Damn! That was four hours ago!'

'I know. But like I said, I took the wrong trail and–'

'All right, all right.'

'Ah Sam, it was terrible. I was out back when it happened. All of a sudden there's this commotion – gunfire, screamin'...' His face screwed up. 'Them sonsofbitches, seems they just walked into the bank, bold as brass, took better'n fifteen thousand dollars at gunpoint, went back out to their horses and high-tailed it up Erdoes Street, firin' their pistols somethin' indiscriminate.'

Sam's fists clenched at his sides. 'Anyone hurt?'

His heart sank even lower when Heck's round head pumped in the affirmative. 'Two. Missus Trotter's eleven-year-old, Victoria...' His voice broke and he palmed his eyes quickly. 'Dead, God rest 'er. And Doc Hobson.'

'Doc?'

'Uh-huh. Hung on for a while. Died just afore Jack sent me out to find you. I tell you, there ain't no justice in this world, Sam

Judge! That little girl … Doc…' He shook his bald head. 'Just in the wrong place at the wrong time…'

Sam swore. Then, while mounting up, he told the butcher about John Redmond, and how he'd been heading back to town to fetch Doc out to see to him. 'Who else you know's had some experience at doctorin'?' he demanded.

Heck, climbing back into his own saddle, gave the question some thought. 'Len Meares,' he said after a while.

'Ostler at the livery?'

'Well, he's had some experience at doctorin' horses an' cattle. I know it ain't exactly the same thing, but–'

'Don't matter, we can't be picky. Minute we get back, go chase 'im up. He might not be able to do much for Redmond, but you never know.'

Heck nodded. 'All right. What about you?'

Sam looked at him, his jaw muscles working something fierce. 'Me? I've got a bank robbery and two killin's to investigate

– and a score to settle with the fellers as did the deed,' he replied.

And one in particular, he added silently as they splashed back across Tom Smith Creek and pushed their animals south toward town.

My son.

Sam knew he'd have guessed something was wrong even if Heck hadn't caught up with him out at the creek. The minute Austin Springs came into sight, he sensed something *dead* about the wood and brick buildings clustered across the Rio Grande's west bank, something indefinable that somehow spoke of shock and mourning.

It made his skin go tight.

They'd done the two-hour ride in ninety minutes. Now it was four-thirty or thereabouts; the better part of six hours since chaos had come a-calling.

Urging their tired mounts on, they entered First at a walk. The street was practically empty, which was pretty much how Sam had expected to find it. Folks were home now, licking their wounds or thanking their stars. He'd seen similar reactions before. What few townspeople he did see refused to meet his gaze for any length of time. It was almost as if *they'd* been responsible for the robbery, and were ashamed of their part in it.

He'd seen that reaction before, too.

As they came to the law office, the sun bleached the blue out of the sky and replaced it with something dark and ominous that promised early nightfall. With a grunt, Sam left Heck to go find Len Meares while he tied Charlie to the hitch-rack and loosened the animal's cinch-strap. Once that was done he went up onto the boardwalk and inside.

Jack O'Neal was in there waiting for him, as was Wallace Corey, the manager of the bank. Both of them were still wearing their smartest business clothes, but even such fine suits and stiff collars looked worn and ragged now, just like the men themselves. As the marshal came through the door, Jack came out of the chair behind the desk, his tanned face haggard.

'Sam! Heck found you all right, then?'

Sam nodded, feeling tired as hell. 'Howdy Jack, Wallace.' To the bank manager he said, 'Your people all right, are they?'

Corey returned his nod. He was forty, of slight physique and greying at the temples and beard. 'Shaken up, as you can imagine,' he replied in his familiar West Virginia drawl. 'But better off than … some…'

'You've wired your head office? Told 'em what happened?'

'Yes. If the money isn't recovered within forty-eight hours, they're issuing a ten percent reward.'

Sam took off his hat and moved around to flop into his creaky chair. It was still warm where the mayor had parked his ass. Almost as soon as he was settled, Mitzi, the fat Abyssinian cat, appeared from nowhere and hopped up onto his lap.

Idly the marshal rubbed at the cat's ears. 'All right,' he said wearily. 'Let's go over it one more time, just so's I've got it all straight in my mind.'

They did, but nothing fresh emerged. Heck Mabey had told it pretty much as it was. Red, the youngster with the black gloves, freckles and snub nose, had done all the talking. The rest had just backed him up.

'Nobody thought to organise a posse and go after 'em, then?' Sam asked when Corey had finished recounting events.

Now seated on the other side of the desk, Jack O'Neal bristled at the implied criticism. 'Well … no. By the time the shock had worn off…'

'All right, all right.'

'But I wired a bulletin to all the towns directly east of here,' the mayor went on, still indignant. 'With any luck, the authorities out that way should catch those bastards – uh, excuse my language, Wallace – inside twenty-four hours.'

Sam reached for the hand-rolled Havana Jack had given him earlier that day. A letter bearing his name and address in a neat but unfamiliar hand had been left beside it, most probably by Jonathan Cook, the clerk down at the U.S. Post Office. He made a mental note to read it as soon as he was able.

'Why send a bulletin east?' he asked as he unwrapped the cigar.

'Huh?'

'What about north, south and west?'

From the expression on Jack's face, the reason was obvious. 'East was the direction those bandits were riding when they left town.'

The marshal struck a match and got the cigar working. 'It didn't occur to you that they might switch direction once they were out on open range, then?'

'Switch...?'

'Forget it, Jack. You're too honest to think sneaky.' He blew a smoke ring. 'Don't matter, anyway. Happen it don't rain tonight, I should pick their trail up at first light tomorrow.'

O'Neal frowned. 'Hold on a minute, Sam! This is out of your hands now – as well you know. The moment those robbers crossed the town limits they were out of your jurisdiction.'

'Granted. But–'

'Hear me out, Sam. And *pay attention*. This is a matter for the county sheriff now, and I've wired him accordingly. With luck he should be here by Sunday.'

'That's as maybe,' Sam replied around the cigar. 'But you're forgettin' somethin', Jack. This is *my* town that they hit, and two of the folks you pay *me* to protect that they killed.' He decided not to mention his more personal interest in the proceedings, and fortunately the shifting veil of fragrant cigar smoke went some of the way towards hiding the fire in his usually-placid grey eyes. 'You think I'm gonna sit back and wait another two days for the county sheriff to get here? You better think again!'

'Sam…' the mayor said sternly.

But Sam's lean, weather-beaten face was set firm. 'I'm goin' after 'em, Jack, with or without this badge,' he said quietly. 'And

I'm gonna get 'em, too.'

There was a moment of silence as they traded stares, watched by an uncomfortable-looking Corey. Then Sam set the cat down and rose. 'Now, if you'll excuse me, I figure to go pay my respects to Sophie Trotter and Doc's ... widow.'

O'Neal watched him pick up his hat and cross to the door, irritated – not for the first time – by the marshal's stubborn streak. 'You can't mean it, Sam. You've been a lawman too long to take the law into your own hands now. Good God, I understand how you feel – we all feel the same way! But don't you see that it's not for you to play executioner? These are modern times, for heaven's sake – you go off with the intention of killing those bandits and you'll be no better than they are!'

His passionate outburst made Sam stop and look at him. *'Kill?'* he repeated, talking around the stogie. 'I think you got it all wrong, Jack. If you remember correctly, I said I was gonna *catch* them boys, not kill 'em.'

63

Relief made O'Neal deflate. 'Well, that's something, I guess.'

'So I should think,' Sam replied agreeably. 'Hell, why should I waste bullets on 'em? Once they stand trial and everyone sees 'em for exactly what they are, the law'll be only too happy to fix 'em for me.' His smile grew cold and forceful. 'Take my word for it, Jack – the law's gonna hang 'em *all*.'

THREE

About an hour later Sam stepped out of Sophie Trotter's neat little plank-built house and with a muted farewell, clapped his hat down over his thinning black-grey hair and strode up the path to the gate. By now it was some time after six o'clock, and sure enough, night was already streaking itself across the bowl of sky above.

Out on the street, the grizzled marshal at

last gave in to a sigh. Visiting the recently-bereaved had never been one of his favourite chores, but this time 'round it had been even worse than usual. Trying to offer words of comfort to Doc Hobson's widow had been hard enough, but visiting with young Vicky Trotter's shattered parents had been downright *harrowing*.

Maybe it was because young Vicky had only been a child, not even twelve years of age; an *innocent* victim in every sense of the term. Or maybe it was because the older Sam got, the harder it became to accept death in *any* form.

Or maybe…

He didn't want to think about it, but he couldn't ignore the possibility.

Maybe it was because it just might have been one of Matt's bullets that'd ended the child's life.

As he stomped back towards the centre of town, the last southbound of the day came hissing into the rail depot about a hundred yards further down the street. Glancing that way, he watched the big shiny Baldwin glide in on a cushion of steam. *Life goes on,* he told himself tiredly. But then his thoughts turned back to Doc Hobson and Vicky Trotter and he added, *for some.*

Hell.

Truth to tell, he didn't know what was troubling him more – the fact that Matt had been involved in the robbery, or his own apparently desperate desire to go after the culprits himself.

Was he really doing it because the robbers had hit *his* town and killed *his* people? Was he doing it because Matt's presence made it even more personal? Or – and this was most likely closest to the truth, he decided – was he doing it because such a manhunt promised to be his last chance of recapturing some of the action and glory of his past?

He chose not to ponder on the answer.

Around him, the streets were still pretty quiet. Every so often a wagon or horseback rider would hurry past, but that was about all. Even the few tinny piano-sounds coming from the Saddle of Faith over on Mitchell

Street seemed half-hearted.

En route to his office he stopped by a general store and bought supplies to see him through the next couple of days; canned foods, a small sack of coffee beans and sweetening, a few strips of jerky and some preserves.

'Goin' huntin', Sam?' asked the elderly storekeeper, as if news of Sam's decision hadn't already circulated around town.

'Somethin' like that,' the marshal replied.

'In that case,' the storekeeper said, indicating the supplies spread across the counter, 'all this is on the house.'

'Huh?'

'Just make them bastards pay for what they done, Sam, that's all I ask.'

Sam gathered his order together, arranging everything in a gunnysack the storekeeper gave him. 'Obliged, Mr Bridges.'

'Don't mention it.'

At the Saddle of Faith – where his entrance caused something of a stir in the otherwise lifeless proceedings – he bought a bottle of cheap whisky. At Yale's Emporium he stocked up on cigars. And at Clint Adams' gunsmith's shop he purchased spare ammunition for the Remington and his old Spencer carbine.

It was around seven, seven-fifteen when he finally got back to the dark and empty office. Setting his purchases down on the desk, he reached out to turn up the guttering lantern hanging from the centre of the ceiling – and heard the faintest of noises behind him.

Figuring that anyone who chose to skulk around in dark corners must be up to no good, he spun with a speed that belied his years, right hand automatically diving to the Army .44. In an instant the long gun was free of leather and coming up to line on the shadowy figure framed inside the door which led through to the cell-block.

The figure raised a hand. 'Don't shoot!'

Sam didn't – but neither did he return the gun to its holster.

There was something about the other

feller's voice that made his short hairs shift in warning. What was it? Sucking in a deep breath, he tightened his hold on the Remington's wooden grips.

Quietly he said, 'That you, Matt?'

The figure made no move at first. Then it came forward a pace, and a stray shaft of light from the gas street-lamp outside caught the boy's youthful but rugged face.

'It's me,' he replied.

Then he collapsed.

Sam slipped the gun back into leather and got the lamp working fast, then hurried over to the sprawled form.

One way or another, it had been a day for shocks, but none of them had prepared him for this. He didn't know what to make of Matt's sudden appearance. Maybe he'd decided to give himself up. Maybe. But whatever the answer, Sam was sure glad to see him – he thought.

In the corner, Mitzi watched with much curiosity as her master lifted the boy gently and carried him back into the cell-block. The lock-up area wasn't much – just a narrow stone corridor formed by two nine-foot-square cells on either side and a barred window high in the end wall. Using one foot, Sam kicked open the first door he came to and set his boy down on the nearest hard bunk. Then he got a lamp working in there too, and hurried back outside to fetch the whisky.

Matt looked as pale as death stretched out on the pallet. Sam uncorked the bottle, lifted the boy's head and spilled some of the fiery liquid across his bloodless lips.

Nothing happened at first; then his efforts were rewarded by a series of coughs and splutters as Matt returned to consciousness. After a moment the boy opened his dazed gunmetal eyes to find Sam crouching beside him, examining him with surprising care.

'…Sam…?'

The lean lawman glanced up at him, his face pinched with a mixture of anger and relief. 'Who did this?' he asked.

Matt swallowed, licking the last of the whisky off his puffed lips. 'That ain't … important…'

'The hell you say! Somebody's worked you over good, boy. Who was it – your precious "friends"? Didn't they like the way fifteen grand split between the six of you?'

Matt closed his eyes again. His voice was pained and thick with emotion. 'You … you got any more of that … rotgut handy?'

Sam shook his head, unable to quell his rising anger. 'No. Not for you.' He clenched one fist and slammed it against the side of the bunk, filling the cell-block with the hum of vibrating springs. 'Just what the hell did you think you were doing, Matt? Dammit, do you know that you and your friends killed two people on your way out of town? The only doctor for thirty miles in any direction and a poor defenceless–'

'*I know!*' Matt cut in, his bruised face contorted with remorse.

Sam watched the tears spill heavily from his son's eyes and felt some of the fury

71

seeping out of him. 'All right,' he said, his tone a shade calmer. 'Let's hear your side of it – not that it'll do you much good. You're in this up to your neck, boy – but I guess you don't need me to tell you that.'

He moved over to the opposite bunk and sat down, keeping his stony expression neutral as the boy tried to ease himself up onto one elbow. 'That's why I came here – to tell my side of it.'

He sighed. 'I don't expect you to believe any of what I'm gonna say. From the looks of it, I'm already guilty as sin as far as you're concerned. Well, believe what you like – I don't care any more. But for what it's worth … I didn't have anything to do with the robbery.'

'*What?*'

'Oh, I knew it was gonna happen. Hell, we'd been plannin' it ever since Duquesne; how we was gonna find a nice little town with a big fat bank and go take ourselves a fortune.' His voice dropped. 'Only then I ran into you.'

'And that gave you second thoughts?' Sam asked sceptically.

Matt winced, whether from pain or criticism Sam couldn't tell. 'Somethin' like that,' the boy replied. 'See, I didn't want to go agin you, Sam. Only a fool would want a run-in with the feller they still mention alongside the likes of Hickok an' Stoudenmire. I said as much to Baylor, too; that maybe we ought to ride on and find another town, or just forget about takin' up the owl-hoot trail altogether.'

'Baylor?'

'Baylor Ryan. The jasper you called Red when you braced us over at the cafe this mornin'.'

Sam nodded. 'All right. Go on.'

'Well, Baylor an' the others agreed – they didn't want no trouble with you either, your reputation bein' what it was. Only what I didn't know was that while me 'n' you was chewin' the fat out there this mornin', Baylor and the rest was chewin' some fat of their own.' His smile came out more like a grimace. 'I guess they started wonderin' just how far they could trust me, seein' as how I was on such neighbourly terms with a badge-packer.'

Sam could guess the rest. 'So they turned on you.'

Matt nodded again. 'Yep. Waited 'til we was about half a dozen miles outside town and then let me have it.' His eyes dropped to the scratched stone floor. *'Bastards.* Ran off my horse and beat me senseless, then left me unconscious a little ways back from the trail an' came back here to go through with … with what we'd been plannin' all along.'

Sam felt a surge of relief that threatened to leave him light-headed. Despite everything, he'd been dreading the prospect of going after his own son. But could Matt be believed? Sam thought so – but knew he must fight hard to remain impartial, to be a lawman first and a father second.

'How come this Baylor didn't injure you more permanent?' he asked. 'Strikes me he'd be a fool to leave you alive, knowin' as how you could identify him an' his cronies so well.'

The younger man shrugged. 'I don't know. Old times' sake? Like I told you before, we travelled quite a set o' miles together, me an' them boys.' His voice turned wistful, and Sam knew he was wishing he was still with them, but back in some earlier, less-complicated time.

'Anyway,' the boy said, running a splay-fingered hand through his curly black hair and feeling for bumps, 'where was I?'

'The robbery.'

'Uh-huh.' Another sigh. 'Well, by the time I come to, it must've been headin' towards noon. I felt pretty rough – guess I still do. Figured to have at least one busted rib. They was good friends, them boys, and we had some good times, too. But let me tell you, there ain't one of 'em shy when it comes to usin' his fists.

'Anyway, I knew that Baylor an' the boys'd most probably turned over the bank by then, or leastways *tried* to, so there was no point in me hustlin' back here to warn anyone. So I just lay where I was, waitin' for the world to stop spinnin' around me. Far as I knew, Baylor an' the rest was either dead or locked up – or ridin' south with their saddle-bags a-bulgin' with money.'

'South? That where you boys figured on headin' once you knocked over the bank?'

'Uh-huh. Straight up across the mountains and down over the state line into New Mexico.'

Sam thought about that, computing distances in his mind. 'All right, go on.'

Matt lay back. 'Not much more to tell. After a while I felt spry enough to start walkin'. By the time I reached the outskirts o' town the whole place was buzzin' with what'd happened – includin' how two locals'd stopped bullets in the getaway.' He swallowed hard, struggling to keep his voice even. 'That was Baylor, of course. He said a volley of gunfire'd leave everyone too spooked to come after us, only it didn't work out that way. So I lay low outside of town, figurin' that if anyone spotted me an' remembered seeing me with the others earlier on, I'd be strung up for sure.'

'Local feelin' bein' what it is, I reckon you figured right. But what in hell made you pick *this* place as your hidey-hole?'

Matt tried to shrug. 'Seemed the safest place.'

Relenting a little, Sam gestured to the whisky bottle beside the bunk. 'All this talkin' must be thirsty work,' he allowed gruffly. 'Go ahead an' oil your tonsils.'

'Thanks.' Matt helped himself, gratefully. The second belt of rye brought some colour back to his cheeks, but he still looked pretty frayed around the edges. He lay back, holding his chest, as the marshal got to his feet.

'Sam?'

'Yeah?'

'...what ... what happens now?'

The voice was young and afraid.

Sam eyed him closely. 'To you, you mean – or your friends?'

'To me.'

He shrugged. 'To be honest with you, boy, I don't know. By rights I guess I should charge you with conspiracy to commit a felony and hold you here for the county sheriff. But because I know you, I'd appreciate to give you a second chance.'

The boy bristled. 'No offence, Sam, but I ain't lookin' for no favours. I'll take whatever's comin' to me.'

Sam smiled, fiercely proud. Rosie'd done a good job dragging this boy up. 'Listen, son. Them lumps 'n' bumps of yours ain't figments of your imagination. Someone *did* beat you up. And happen I ask Wallace Corey how many *hombres* robbed his bank, it's my expectation that he'll say five, an' not the six I kinda took for granted. Besides which, you had nothin' to gain by comin' back here if your story wasn't true.' He shook his head, lowered his voice. 'Far as I'm concerned, the only mistake you made was gettin' in with the wrong crowd. And if you meant what you said about givin' up the idea of ridin' the owlhoot…'

'I did. It was a damn-fool notion anyway.'

'Then I figure you deserve a second chance.'

They looked at each other across the lamplit cell. 'First thing I gotta do is go round up Jack O'Neal an' tell him as much as I think he needs to know,' Sam explained. 'Then I aim to put the whole business to Abe Warren, the local J.P, an' swear a deposition as to your innocence in the matter.'

'You think that'll turn the trick?'

'Why in hell shouldn't it? You're blameless, boy. And by the time I've finished tellin' as how you tried to stop them other fellers from doin' what they did, you'll be lucky if these locals don't hail you as a hero.'

Anxiety washed away from Matt's face as his muscles relaxed. 'Thanks, *amigo*.'

'Don't thank me, boy. You're gonna *earn* your freedom – firstly by walkin' the straight an' narrow from this point on, an' secondly by tellin' me everythin' you can about your "friends", up to an' includin' their plans for after the robbery.'

Matt's reply was a grim nod. 'You'll get it all,' he said softly. *'Everythin'.* I promise.'

It was all somewhat irregular, to say the least, as even Sam himself had to confess as he explained events first to Jack O'Neal and then to Justice of the Peace Abner C. Warren. But the ageing marshal told the story with such conviction that by eight-thirty the lay magistrate had signed his deposition, and in the eyes of the law, Matthew Prescott Dury was as innocent as the proverbial newborn babe.

After that Sam hurried back to the office, fetching with him bandages and carbolic with which to patch Matt up. The boy dozed while he cooked some beans on the old office range, but woke up just in time to accept the proffered plate.

Then came the business of interrogation.

Sam wanted to know everything; names, histories, habits, quirks, weaponries, weaknesses. Matt told him as much as he could.

Outside, in the darkened main office, the hands of the big yellow-faced clock moved slowly from nine o'clock to nine-forty-five. By ten Matt's eyelids were drooping again and Sam decided to call it a night.

Seated behind the desk in the shadowy office, a cheap cigar glowing between his teeth and Mitzi curled up asleep on his lap, the marshal reviewed everything he'd learned.

Imprinted on his mind were five names – Baylor Ryan; Raul Sadillo; Lester Hayes; Jim Dalton; Art Casey. Beside each name was a description – the redhead with freckles across his snub nose; the dark, pocked face of the Mexican with the thin, rat's-tail moustache along his upper lip; the slab-shouldered black boy in the broadcloth jacket; the sharp-faced, whippy youngster with the cruel Spanish colonial spurs on his high-heeled boots; and the short, lardy blond with the weak jaw and cross-draw holster.

Five names. Five faces.

He blew a smoke ring, thinking about Doc Hobson and Vicky Trotter.

With any luck, five customers for the hang-man.

'Damn you, Baylor!'

Art Casey ran one sausage-fingered hand across his red, sweaty face and planted his feet firmly in an aggressive and challenging stance.

He and his four comrades had finally called a halt in their hell-for-leather flight from Austin Springs. They were up in the foothills of the Sangre de Christos now, about thirty-five, forty miles to the south, surrounded by weathered pines and aspen, sagebrush ten feet tall, lichen, wild flowers, thick grass and rocks the colour of rust, about as safe from pursuit as they were likely to get.

'You hear me, Baylor?'

There had been little time for talk during the last ten hours. In those few times they had called a brief halt to spell the heaving horses, the five boys had been too winded themselves for conversation. But now...

Now a moonless night had claimed the land, making it impossible for them to ride further with any degree of safety or confidence.

With no other option, Baylor had called a halt. Lester and Raul had put up a makeshift corral; Jim had taken his Winchester and back-tracked a ways to stand first watch on the trail. And Art Casey had finally found breath enough to brace Baylor Ryan at long last.

'You got somethin' to say, Art, you come right out and say it,' Ryan suggest easily.

Casey swallowed. Some little way off, unbuckling cinch-straps and lifting saddles from the backs of their lathery horses, the Negro and the Mexican watched curiously.

Casey was a fleshy twenty-four-year-old with a mole-dotted face, clear blue eyes and an ill-tempered twist to his thick, spittle-flecked lips. A native of Sheffield, Texas, he suffered from a temperament that was as impulsive as it was immature. Moody and self-centred, Casey could always be relied upon to bitch about something. At the moment, however, he seemed more determined than usual.

'Oh, I intend to, don't worry,' he replied, calming somewhat. 'I'm talkin' about that little girl, damn you.'

Baylor Ryan frowned. 'What little girl? What you flappin' about?'

'You mean you never even *saw* her? That itty-bitty little girl you shot on the way outta town?'

Ryan's round, freckled face betrayed nothing. 'I don't know what you're talkin' about, Art,' he replied quietly. 'I didn't shoot anyone. None of us did.'

'*Someone* did,' Casey insisted grimly. 'Oh, sure. Fire over their heads, you said. But I still saw that kid go down 'neath your gun, Bay. You might've crippled her, for God's sake! Why, for all we know she could even be dead!' His face screwed up into a baby-like mask.

'Ah, you're lettin' your imagination run away with you,' Ryan said disparagingly. 'You're bushed, Art. We all are. It's been a long day.' He forced a smile. 'But a profitable one, eh?'

Casey shook his head. 'She could be dead…' he insisted.

Hayes, the Negro, came over in a series of loose-limbed strides. Sweat still covered his wide, flat face, and left a dark, damp stain around the sweatband of his curl-brimmed Stetson. 'He right,' he told Ryan in his deep Southern accent. 'Ah saw the girl go down mahself. Middle-age' man as well.'

Ryan faced them both with anger stiffening his expression. He hadn't wanted to make a big thing out of this; Lord knew, these fellers were already spooked enough as it was. But now it seemed that he had no option.

What was it his uncle used to say, back home in the dry Great Basin country of Nevada? 'You don't fry an egg without you crack it first.' Why couldn't these *hombres* see that? Nothing is for nothing; everything has a price.

'All right!' he snapped. 'So a couple of townies got in the way. But happen you fellers don't want to hang, you'll remember what I just now told you. *I* didn't shoot *anyone. None* of us did.'

Silence filled the clearing. Over by the horses, Raul Sadillo watched the trio closely through dark, bead-like eyes.

'You got that?' Ryan barked.

Hayes nodded slowly. 'Ah guess. Too late to do anythin' about it now, anyway.'

But Casey wasn't finished. 'You wasn't aimin' over their heads, Bay,' he said dreamily, as if he was just putting all his thoughts together for the first time. 'You was aimin' at *them.*'

Ryan's face darkened. 'What? *What?* That's a hell of a thing to say, Casey! Was we any-place else, I'd take you to task over it, don't you fret! But...' His voice softened, but only with effort. 'Look, this is no time for us to fall out now. We got to stick together.'

Again Hayes said, 'Ah guess.'

The freckle-faced leader of the young guns studied Casey closely. The fat boy looked just about beat in his clammy grey check shirt and creased levis. Even the coffee-brown sugarloaf sombrero atop his long, straw-coloured hair seemed somehow bedraggled. But for once, his weak jaw was set firm.

'Leave my nag as she is, Raul,' he called over his shoulder. 'I'm ridin' on.'

'Now listen here, Art–'

Casey took a step forward, rage plain in his eyes. 'No – *you* listen. Don't it bother you fellers that we might've killed a couple of people back in that town? That they might be printin' murder warrants for us right now?' He took a pace away again. 'I've finished with you boys, all of you. I don't even want my share of the lousy money.' Again he glanced over his shoulder at the Mexican, then back at the Negro, then back to Ryan. 'I used to think we made a good crew, Baylor. I was proud to ride with you-all. But I figure the rot set in when we beat up on poor ole Matt.' He shook his head, his expression sad and disgusted. 'Turnin' on one of our own, that was bad enough … but shootin' little kids without even a smidgin o' regret…'

'Art…' Ryan's voice held a note of warning that Casey didn't fail to pick up. 'You can't run out on us now, buddy. Like I said, we got to stick together.'

Casey shook his head. 'I'm leavin', whether you like it or not, Bay. Don't worry, though, I'll ride careful – I'm no more anxious to get my neck stretched than you are. But even if I *do* get arrested, I won't tell on you. Any of you. You got my word on it.'

Lester Hayes said, 'Where you figger to go, Art?'

But before he could reply, Ryan said, 'Nowhere.'

'Huh?'

As Casey's blue eyes returned to him, Ryan's black-gloved right hand flexed ominously above the grips of his Colt's Peacemaker.

'Hey, come on now—'

'Stand clear, Les. If Art wants to ride out, let 'im. But he'll have to put me down first.'

The pudgy blond paled as his troubled gaze travelled up from Ryan's gun hand to his face. There was fear in him now, but still more than a little defiance.

'So it comes to this, does it?' he asked after clearing his throat.

Ryan nodded slowly. 'Yep.'

The tree-fringed clearing fell quiet.

'I won't fight you, Bay.'

Ryan sneered. 'You want to ride out of here, you're gonna have to.'

Casey glanced down at the Smith & Wesson Schofield resting butt-forward in the cross-draw holster at his left hip. He flexed his own right hand, but made no move to reach for the weapon.

'Bay…'

'You backin' down then, Art? Seein' sense at last?'

The silence was deafening. Casey swallowed again, hard, causing his Adam's apple to dance briefly. After a moment he licked his lips and shook his head.

'Nope,' he replied regretfully. 'I ain't backin' down.'

'Right,' Ryan said, suddenly stiffening. 'Then *draw!*'

The two boys went for their guns. Both of them were pretty fast, but one was just a fraction faster than the other. The silence exploded to the sound of a gunshot, followed quickly by a scream.

Lester Hayes winced. Raul Sadillo reached out to calm the restless horses surrounding him.

Baylor Ryan buckled to the ground, clutching his bloody right arm. 'I'm hit! Damn it, I'm hit! The bastard *drilled* me!' His voice was high and panicky, his words punctuated by pain-racked sobs.

Art Casey was still locked in the crouch from which he had fired his shot. If anything, he looked even paler now than he had before the confrontation. Up until now, Baylor had always been reckoned as the faster gun. Maybe he still was. Maybe Art had just got lucky. Since he'd actually been aiming for Baylor's chest, he was inclined to think so. But whichever it was, the lardy blond had no intention of sticking around to push that luck to its limits.

He snapped out of the trance and put his gun away, turning to approach the horses on legs like jelly.

'*You bastard!*' Baylor cried from somewhere behind him, 'Les ... Raul ... stop him. *Stop him!*'

But Les and Raul made no move to stop Art from cutting his dun gelding from the makeshift rope corral and re-securing his loosened cinch-strap with thick, trembling fingers. They hated to admit it, but Art had been right. Beating up poor ole Matt had been a hell of a thing to do. They weren't about to do it again to another of their number.

On the ground about twenty feet away, Ryan tried to pick up his fallen Peacemaker with numb fingers. 'Get him, Raul!'

Calm as a sea breeze now, sensing that he was no longer under any immediate threat, Art Casey stepped up to leather and touched the brim of his hat in farewell. Then he wheeled the dun around and headed back down the trail, off into the night.

A moment later, Jim Dalton came running, his long-rowelled spurs jingling musically. His Winchester was held at the ready, his sharp, dark-eyed face both puzzled and fearful. 'What is it? What's happened? I heard a gunshot, then I passed Art ridin' out—'

He pulled up short at the sight of Lester Hayes cutting Ryan's bloody shirtsleeve away from the messy shoulder wound.

'Holy Mother of God, what happened here?' he gasped.

It was Raul Sadillo who answered him. Still watching the shadows which had swallowed up Art Casey, he said, 'The rot.'

'Huh?'

'The rot,' he repeated. 'It jus' set in.'

FOUR

The town marshal of Long Branch, Colorado, was sitting in his office with his boots up on the desk, shooting the breeze with his lanky deputy, when the fat Abyssinian cat slid through the partially-open door and sashayed across the timber floor to leap up onto his desk.

'Huh?' George W. Murphy's chocolate-brown eyes widened in surprise as the cat let out a plaintive *meow*. As he straightened up in his seat, sunlight bounced off the shield on his broad chest. 'Where the hell did *you* come from?'

'Austin Springs,' Sam Judge replied, appearing in the sun-filled doorway. 'Mind if I come in?'

Since he was already closing the door behind him, the question was more than a mite academic. But Murphy, who was a big-bellied man in his forties with a full brown beard falling down to the third button of his blue cotton shirt, said, 'Sure. Do somethin' for you? Saucer of milk for your cat, maybe?'

Ignoring the sarcasm, Sam reached into the pocket of his fringed buckskin jacket and brought out his own star. 'Name's Judge. Town law for Austin Springs.'

'Murphy,' Murphy said, rising to shake hands. 'This here is my assistant, Henry Davies.' Davies – tall, skinny, pale and reserved – also shook. 'Quite a ways from Austin Springs, ain't you?'

'That I am,' Sam agreed, glancing around the dark office, which mirrored his own in all but disarray. 'Thing is, we had a little trouble about four days ago. Our branch of the Colorado State Bank was robbed.'

'You don't say. How much they get away with?'

'Better'n fifteen thousand.'

Murphy whistled. *'Oooh* boy.'

Sam shrugged. 'Well, that on its own wouldn't've been so bad. Banks carry insurance, just like everyone else. But on their way out of town, the five bastards who did the deed shot an' killed two people. Three, if you count a rancher whose health was kind of reliant on him gettin' a visit from our only doctor, who was one of said victims.'

'That's bad,' said Murphy, frowning. 'Pull up a chair, Judge. Henry, go pour the marshal a mug o' java, will you?'

'Black an' sweet, if you got it.'

'Sure.'

While Henry went to pour, Sam continued talking with Mitzi circling his feet in an aimless, restless pattern. He'd intended to leave the cat back home, such creatures being a hindrance on a manhunt, but stubbornly she'd followed him so far beyond the town limits that he'd had no choice but to bring her along. And to be fair, she'd been no trouble. She was quite happy, in fact, to travel tucked into one of his saddle-bags, with only her big, pointy-eared head visible.

'Just to put you in the picture,' Sam explained, watching life go by in an endless variety of permutations beyond the room's single barred window, 'I've taken a couple weeks' leave of absence to go after these here varmints myself. Been trailin' 'em through the mountains for the past few days. Got a pretty fair notion as to where it is they're headed, too, but the trail's been coolin' off somewhat. I wondered if maybe they stopped by here to resupply, Long Branch not bein' too far off their route.'

The bearded marshal gave that some thought, sucking at his gappy, yellowed teeth. 'Well, it's true that I *do* try an' keep an eye on everyone who passes through town, but Long Branch bein' a little less settled than Austin Springs, that ain't allus possible. You got a description of these robbers?'

'Uh-huh. Names to fit the faces, too,' Sam replied. As the deputy handed him a steaming enamel mug, he ran through the details Matt had given him, but at the end of it, Murphy only shook his head.

'Don't sound familiar at all. Henry?'

The deputy shrugged his narrow shoulders. 'Nope. I'd of remembered a bunch like that, I think.'

Sam sipped the coffee, glancing back through the window at the busy street outside. 'That don't mean they couldn't be here, though, right?'

'Right,' said Murphy. 'Like I told you, we see new faces out on them streets ever' day of the week, prospectors, miners or representatives of some of the bigger minin' companies from back East. But there's an awful lot more that we don't never see. Could be the boys you're after are among 'em. My advice is to ask a round some of the stores an' saloons.'

Sam nodded. 'That was my intention. Jus' thought I might save myself some time stoppin' by here first.'

Murphy rose again. 'Well, I wish you luck, Judge. Sounds like you got your work cut out for you.'

Sam finished his coffee and set the mug

down on the edge of the desk. When he rose also, the other lawman offered his hand again. Halfway through the shake, however, Marshal Murphy increased his grip noticeably.

'Just one last thing afore you go,' he said in a low voice. 'I know who you are, Judge – I mean, who you *really* are. What was it they used to call you – "King Of The Town-Tamers" wasn't it? Well, despite what you might've heard contrary-wise, Long Branch is a peaceful little burg. If you spot the men you're lookin' for here in town, you'll refrain from sparkin' off any trouble or you'll answer to me. I don't mind a nice quiet arrest, but a shootin'-match I can do without. And don't forget, you're on leave of absence, *marshal*. Got no legal authority here at all.'

Sam met the other man's stare and smiled, pulling his hand free. 'Fair enough,' he said amiably. 'But now that you've had *your* say, I'll have mine; and since I don't chew my cabbage twice, Murphy, you'd best pin your ears back an' listen up sharp.'

'*What?*'

'I'm here to find five men an' take 'em in to stand trial for robbery an' murder, not restart the Civil War,' Sam told him evenly. 'If I've got anythin' to do with it, these jaspers'll have their day in court, just like anyone else. But happen they decide different an' try to make a fight of it, I'll fight back. You got *that?*'

Murphy coloured quickly. 'I never said nothin' about not defendin' yourself,' he muttered sullenly.

'No,' Sam agreed. 'But just so's you know.' He nodded to the deputy. 'Thanks for the coffee, Davies, it was right welcome. Come on, Mitz, let's make tracks.'

Obediently the cat followed her master out onto the street.

Long Branch was a medium-sized town that had sprung up amidst the towering Sangre de Christos to cater mainly for the mining industry which had been lured to the mountains by the promise of silver.

Constructed at the westernmost point of the Purgatoire River, the town boasted – among other things – four saloons, two hotels, a Catholic church, barbershop, general stores, billiard halls, a combination doctor/dentist, undertaker, a school, several boarding-houses, restaurants, a dressmaker and even a rarely-used theatre.

Residential dwellings had been built further back from the main stem, so that they ringed the busy commercial district. Sam had seen them during his descent into the bowl of verdant land that accommodated the place. But although some of the houses had a solid, permanent look to them, he had noticed a number of others – from basic ten-by-twelve cabins to more ambitious two-and-three-bedroomed structures – that he had immediately recognised as prefabricated homes of the type mailed out across the country by companies like Lyman Bridges in Chicago.

Straightaway he'd seen the benefit of living

in such accommodation, for as soon as the silver petered out (as inevitably it must), all a body had to do was unscrew his four walls and a roof, lash it tightly aboard a decent-sized wagon and then move on to pastures a-fresh.

Back out on Main now, the ageing marshal paused to plant his old round-crowned Stetson back atop his thinning black-grey hair. It was around the dinner hour, and after seventy-two hours of trail-chow, he was kind of keen to savour some good home cooking.

Deciding to put Charlie, his strawberry roan, up at the first livery he came to and go find a beanery before beginning his search of the town, he bent, scooped up the cat and shoved her unceremoniously into his left-side saddle-bag. Then he untied his reins from the hitch-rack outside the law office and mounted up. Soon he had joined the flow of traffic headed east along Main.

It had been as he was preparing Charlie for the first leg of his journey in the cool, early-morning chill of the Erdoes Street

Livery that he'd learned the news of John Redmond's passing. Len Meares, a usually cheerful sixty-year-old who helped out around the stable and did odd-jobs for people like Wallace Corey, had been seated in the small office out back of the livery, seeing only the half-empty bottle of Jim Beam on the desk in front of him.

At once Sam had felt a mild electric tingle wash through him. When he'd left Heck Mabey the previous afternoon, the bald butcher had been going to hunt up Meares, who was a passable vet, to see if he could do anything for the horse-rolled rancher.

It was obvious from his manner, however, that he hadn't. Mourning was written all over him.

'Len?'

Meares didn't hear him at first. The second time Sam used his name he looked up. His eyes were dull and bloodshot, from drink or tears of failure, he couldn't say.

'He's dead, Sam, Redmond, I mean. I...' His voice trailed off.

The ageing lawman had set his weight against the narrow doorway leading from the stable to the office. *Damn.* 'I kind of expected it,' he replied quietly. 'But I guess there was always the chance.'

Meares nodded. 'Oh, sure. He was a strong man, that Redmond. A fighter. If Doc'd been there, things might've worked out different. But … hell, I probably helped the poor devil on his way, what with all my proddin' and probin'.'

'Who's lookin' after his widow?' Sam asked.

But Meares was still thinking about Redmond himself … 'just slipped away…' he said distantly. 'Right in front of me … just passed right on…'

'Len, I as' you a question. Who's takin' care of his missus?'

The ostler focused on him at last. 'Who…? Oh, Heck Mabey. He brought her back with us last night. Said his wife'd look after her 'til she was over the worst of it.'

Sam nodded. 'Good. She'll be in steady

hands there.'

'I guess.'

After that he went back to saddling up. But he wasn't about to forget what Meares had said. *If Doc'd been there, things might've worked out different.*

Doc Hobson. Vicky Trotter. *John Redmond.*

However indirectly, it was just one more reason to go after the boys who'd brought carnage to his town.

Sam left Charlie at a clean and busy stable next door to a three-storey hotel with a false front that seemed to scratch the sky, and much to the amusement of the stable-boy, solemnly told Mitzi to stay put and not wander.

'Where can a man buy some decent vittles around here, friend?' he asked as he paid for two hours' worth of board for the roan.

'Lizzie Edwards' place, four doors along,' came the reply. 'As home cookin' goes, she takes a lot o' beatin'.'

'Thanks.'

Sam collected his change and stepped back outside, there to pause while he fished a cigar from his inside pocket and bit off the end. He struck a vesta, got the match half-way to the end of the cigar – and froze. *Because over on the opposite boardwalk was Art Casey.*

Sam's first instinct was to dodge back into the livery. After all, although they'd only seen him the once, he didn't know how well Ryan and his cronies might remember him. But from the look of him, Art Casey – and it *was* Art Casey, right down to the distinctive cross-draw holster – was too preoccupied to notice much of anything.

Sam stayed where he was, trying to figure out where the boy's four friends might be. The likeliest prospect was that they'd holed up somewhere outside of town and sent one of their number in to pick up some supplies.

So, in order to find the others, all he had to do was follow Casey.

Wasn't it? Unless…

Unless they'd split up after the robbery. They hadn't been planning to, according to Matt (whom he'd left recuperating back in the Springs), but maybe there'd been a change of plan.

'Ouch!'

Startled by the sudden, burning pain in his thumb and forefinger, he shook the lighted match out and tossed it away. There was no time to enjoy a smelly cigar now, nor savour a home-cooked meal either. He had other business that needed tending.

The pulses at his temples began to quicken as he crossed the street and followed Casey, watching the plump young blond dodge shoppers on his way along the plankwalk. Again he was struck by the air of preoccupation the boy seemed to give off. What – if anything – did that signify?

Casey took his first left. Sam did likewise. Only about sixty feet separated them. Then Casey turned into a long and narrow general store and Sam slowed his pace before finally coming to a halt altogether.

General store…

As townsfolk flowed in a steady stream around him, he decided that he'd been right first time. Casey was in town buying supplies for his companions, who were probably camped someplace outside of Long Branch, awaiting his return.

He wondered what he should do about it.

His initial impulse was to go in after the bank robber and arrest him straightaway, then knock a few answers out of him in the privacy of George Murphy's jailhouse. But he didn't want to brace Casey in a crowded area. From what Matt had told him, the young gun was impulsive, something of a hothead. Could be his nerves were still stretched taut from the robbery. He might turn around as soon as he heard Sam step through the door behind him, panic, go for iron and turn a simple arrest into a massacre.

The tall lawman swore.

Then an idea struck him. What if he was to brace Casey from the direction he least expected it? Out back of the store, just as he turned to leave with his arms full of purchases?

It sounded good. But first, he had to find a back way *into* the place.

It was a two-storey structure with a set of fire stairs nailed onto the west-side wall that led – according to a weathered shingle – up to the office of an attorney called Jerome T. Clairborne.

At the rear of the store he found a narrow half-glass door at the head of three sagging steps and two larger portals set back from a modest loading-bay. Glancing around to make sure he was unobserved, he put his face to the dusty glass and peered inside. He saw boxes, barrels and bolts of cloth. As he'd suspected, the door opened into a store-room.

Straightening to his full height again, he took a deep breath, reached for the handle and twisted.

The door opened with a soft click.

Trusting folk, these mountain-dwellers, he thought with a twitching smile.

Gently he swung the door inward. It creaked slightly, but not enough to be heard above the small-town pleasantries being exchanged by the storekeeper and his female customer out front.

Sam closed the door behind him.

The storeroom was large and cluttered, dusty and grey. He stood still for a moment, forcing his fast, shallow breathing back to a deeper, steadier rate. Silently he thumbed the leather thong off the hammer of his Remington .44 and slipped the long, heavy handgun from its holster.

He crossed the storeroom quickly, heading for the threadbare curtain that led out into the store itself, pausing once when his boot pressed hard on a loose floorboard, sending out a soft, splintery mouse-squeak.

Then he was over to the curtain, where he narrowed his eyes and peered through the gap.

Shelves packed with a thousand and one odd items stretched from floor to ceiling on both sides of the store. In his first quick scan he saw hats, cloth, shoes, candies, pots, pans, coveralls, flour and brushes. Here was a stack of Blanke's Mojav Coffee, there a pile of Union Leader Cut Plug. Still more comestibles were stacked beneath pilfer-proof glass showcases on the counter, which lay directly ahead. In the centre of the room sat a slim stove with a long funnel stretching up to disappear through the ceiling. Art Casey was standing right beside it.

'Thank you, Mrs Brewer, and a good day to you.'

The storekeeper was young and black-haired, in a green eyeshade and armbands. The woman he'd been addressing, Mrs Brewer, was middle-aged and sober-faced, wearing a lilac dress with matching hat. She nodded to the storekeeper, shed years with a smile, and carrying her provisions, turned and clomped out in black, high-button shoes.

When she was gone, the storekeeper turned his attention to Casey. 'Yes sir, how can I help you?'

Casey had been looking at candy in the jars behind the pilfer-proof glass. 'Ah, yeah. Gimme a couple airtights o' beans, one o' peaches … 'nother o' tomatoes … sack o' Bull Durham an' a slab o' baker's chocolate.' As an afterthought he added, 'Couple pennies-worth of horehound drops, while you're at it.'

Behind the curtain, Sam frowned. Sounded to him like Casey was buying supplies for one man alone. In which case, it looked as if the bank robbers *had* split up after all.

'There you go, mister,' said the store-keeper, putting Casey's purchases into a paper sack. Quickly he tallied the bill, named the figure and accepted five dollars in coin. Sam watched him ring up a total on the heavy iron cash register, scoop out some change and hand it over. 'Call again.'

Casey nodded without much enthusiasm and lifted the sack into his arms. 'Thanks.'

He turned and took three paces toward the exit before Sam came through the curtain with his Remington raised.

'That's far enough, Casey! Just stay right where you are!'

The storekeeper turned, his young face white and indignant. 'What? Who…? What do you think you're–'

'Law,' Sam growled, keeping his eyes on Casey's stiff back. 'Here to make an arrest.'

That was all Casey needed to hear. With a wail that sounded very much like *'No!'* he dropped the bag and spun, his right hand streaking across his paunchy belly to haul his S&W from leather.

Sam muttered a cuss-word and levelled the Remington, figuring to put his quarry out of action with a shoulder-shot. But before he could squeeze trigger, Casey fired twice. Two neat stacks of No 999 Steamboat playing-cards jumped off the shelf beside Sam's head. He flinched and dropped to his knees. For about four seconds the gun-thunder rendered him deaf as a post; then he became aware of Casey's heavy footfalls against the floor and came back up from behind the counter just as Casey disappeared out the door.

With a grunt Sam hustled around the counter and after the younger man. Behind him the irate storekeeper snatched up two ruined decks of cards and shouted, 'What about these, then, huh? Who's going to pay for *them?*'

Sam made it to the boardwalk just in time to see Art legging it across the street without a backward glance. Braving the heavy wagon traffic, he started after the fleeing robber. But something told him pursuit wasn't going to be easy. He was forty-five now, and couldn't remember the last time he'd had to run after *anything.* And the high mountain air, thin as a lawman's bankroll, shrivelled his lungs something cruel. Almost as soon as he began to run he started a stitch.

Those folks near enough to have heard and recognized the gunblasts had scattered to make way for the hunter and the hunted. Sam was dimly aware of screaming and the alarmed cries of men. One woman fainted as he sped past, waving his Remington about to keep his path clear.

About a hundred feet ahead, Art Casey was covering the wrinkly ground pretty fast for a man with a gut on him. He looked back once; Sam saw his pale, mole-speckled face, his clear blue eyes, his thick, twisted lips. Then Casey stumbled and panicked, loosed off another wild shot.

Sam hugged dirt. Nearby a horse reared, spilling its black-suited rider into a water-trough. More screaming; more yelling; Casey increasing the gap between them.

Sam came back to his feet, yelling for Casey to '*Stop!*'

But Casey didn't stop. He had no intention of stopping.

Sam raised his pistol and fired skyward. Casey stumbled again, expecting a white-hot slap of lead in his back. When nothing happened he kept running. With another colourful curse, Sam followed on, wheezing like a rain-filled accordion.

Around a corner, back onto Main.

Sam had a blurred view of wagons, horses,

pale, frightened faces, a hundred different sounds coming at him in a flash-flood of noise. He pulled up sharp, back-stepped before a rattling Conestoga could turn him into dogmeat, then hurried across the street after his quarry.

Deciding that Casey was up to no good, a hefty young man with brown hair and a grey claw-hammer coat stepped into his path and yelled for him to stop. Without breaking stride, Casey pistol-whipped him viciously, causing the fellow's lady-friend to scream and swoon. Then Casey puffed down a narrow alleyway, now obviously nursing a stitch of his own.

Sam leapt up onto the boardwalk and thundered after him, past the bloodied man who was fanning his derby in his girlfriend's face. He was just about to pursue Casey into the alley, when the thin air was again shattered by a gunshot. Sam ducked as splinters exploded from the wall just above his head. Turning, he saw Deputy Henry Davies on the opposite corner, his Colt still smoking in his fist.

At once the ageing lawman's expression darkened. 'Don't shoot at me!' he roared, indicating the alley-mouth with an angry wave. 'Shoot at *him!*'

Before he could berate the deputy further, he heard a crash and a cry. Quickly he eased along the wall and peered around the corner. In his haste, Art Casey had fallen across half a dozen garbage-pails about thirty feet away, and was just now regaining his feet.

Sam planted himself in the mouth of the alley and raised the Remington fast, firing again into the air.

'That's far enough, Casey! You hear me? The next bullet's got your name on it!'

Casey heard him all right. But he was too desperate to take heed. His face contorted into a screaming mask and he thrust his S&W barrel-first in Sam's direction. But before he could fire, Sam snap-aimed and triggered the Remington again.

This time he meant business.

Casey screamed and fell onto his back, dropping his gun in order to clutch at the red wound in his left leg, about eight inches or so above the knee.

Sam hurried up to the fallen boy, still wheezing, and quickly kicked the S&W out of his reach. Casey was wailing so loud that the man from Austin Springs knew he wouldn't hear him, but he said it anyway.

'I told you the next one had your name on it.' Then he lifted his voice so that even the shamefaced Deputy Davies and a throng of other gawkers crowded in the alley-mouth could hear him add, 'Art Casey – in case you haven't guessed it by now, I hereby arrest you in the name of the law!'

To his credit, Casey's first question upon regaining consciousness after the local sawbones dug Sam's slug out of his leg ninety minutes later concerned Vicky Trotter.

'Th ... the girl...' he husked, bleary-eyed and pale-faced. 'What hap ... happened to the girl...?'

Town Marshal George W. Murphy's big, bearded face disappeared from his line of vision. A second later Sam's took his place. 'She died,' he said without preamble.

Art closed his eyes again, screwed them tight shut, muttered the name of the Devil's lair. 'That's what I was afeared of,' he said a while later.

He was stretched out in a cold, grey cell out back of Murphy's office. Sam had asked if he could keep Art there until he passed through this way again, hopefully with the remainder of the bank robbers in tow. Murphy had been only too willing to say yes, figuring it was the least he could do since in all the excitement his deputy had shot at Sam by mistake.

Now the young blond looked from Sam to Murphy, from Murphy to Davies, standing in the cell doorway, then back to Sam.

'They gonna hang me?' he asked in a level tone.

'I reckon,' Sam replied. 'But the court might show some leniency happen I tell 'em you decided to indulge in a little co-operation while you was here.'

Art licked his dry lips. 'You mean like tell-in' you where … where Baylor an' the others is headed?'

'That's what I mean,' Sam said with a nod. 'Well?'

Art was silent.

'You boys split up,' Sam prompted, making it sound more like a statement than a question.

'Uh-huh.'

'Why?'

The youngster smiled without mirth. 'None o' your damn' business.'

'Now see here–' Murphy began angrily, taking a step back towards the wounded prisoner.

Sam's raised hand stopped him. 'The others,' he persisted. 'They still headed for Linarez, down across the New Mexico border?'

Art's blue eyes flashed. 'You been talkin' to Matt,' he said.

'Nope,' Sam replied quietly. 'Matt's been talkin' to *me*. An' it paid him to do so, Art.'

'I'm glad,' the youngster admitted sincerely. 'Matt's a good feller. Went against the grain to beat up on 'im like we did.'

'What happened to the others, Casey?' Murphy interjected. 'You might's well know, we've found your horse and been through your saddle-bags. You're not carryin' any of the money you stole from that bank, so where is it? You bury it? Or–'

Art stifled a drowsy, post-operative yawn. 'You'll get nothin' out o' me, marshal. I promised. Gave my word.'

'To a bunch o' child-killers?' asked Sam.

Silence. Stubborn, ornery silence.

Sam sighed, his gentle grey eyes lifting to the small window high in the stone wall ahead. Craning his neck, Art followed his line of vision, focusing on the bar of dying daylight slanting in to form a sharp square on the dusty floor.

'Man doesn't realise how precious his days are until he ain't got any left,' the lean lawman said meaningfully. Then he re-focused on Art, and Art flinched from the intensity of his gaze. 'Don't you understand, boy? I'm tryin' to give you a chance to save yourself! Was I you, I'd take it, too. Couple years in prison ain't nowhere near as bad as dancin' on air with a length o' hemp just a-tightenin' and a-tightenin' around your throat, shuttin' off your breath an' turnin' you blue!'

They traded stares for a moment, but Sam saw no fear in Casey's eyes. 'Think about it,' he concluded tiredly. 'I'll be leavin' Long Branch at sun-up tomorrow. You got 'til then to decide iffen you want to live or die.'

He turned and was about to walk out when Art's chilly laugh stopped him. He spun back.

'Maybe you didn't hear me the first time,' Art said when he had Sam's full attention again. 'I tol' you, marshal – I promised them boys that I wouldn't tell no tales on 'em, and I aim to keep my word. But more'n' that...' His eyes lost their shine, his mouth pinched down, his bottom lip quivered, his fists bunched the coarse woollen blanket beneath him and his defiant mask slipped just a fraction. 'More'n that,' he repeated softly, 'killin' that little girl, it's just about the worst thing a body could ever do in his whole life. I want to pay for that, marshal. Now that it's come to it, I want to pay so bad I can almost taste it.

'You understand what I'm sayin'?' he asked, struggling to sit upright. 'You can't threaten me with all your talk of hangin'. After what we done, I *want* to hang, marshal.' The words escaped again through gritted teeth. *'I want to hang!'*

FIVE

It was around four p.m. when Sam quit Murphy's office; too late to move on even if he'd felt like it.

At the livery stable he paid a little more

towards overnight board for the strawberry roan and collected Mitzi from where she'd curled up in a warm, hay-filled corner. Carrying the cat under one arm and his saddle-bags over the other, he headed for the lodging-house Marshal Murphy had recommended.

'I'll be by again in the mornin',' Sam had told him as they said their goodbyes at the door. 'See if Casey's changed his mind at all.'

Murphy nodded. 'All right. But I think you better prepare yourself for a disappointment, Judge. I've seen fellers like that 'un afore, so darn grief-struck that they'd hang them*selves* if they could, without waitin' fer a trial.'

Privately, Sam agreed. The determination he'd seen in Art Casey's eyes spoke volumes, and he had no doubt that the boy meant exactly what he'd said. In his passion, his need to pay for his part in Vicky Trotter's death swamped even the natural fear *all* men have of death.

So it was a moody and physically spent Sam Judge who made his way along Isaac Street twenty minutes later, searching for the house George Murphy had mentioned.

''Afternoon.'

Sam stopped squinting at the neat, affluent-looking clapboard and stone-built houses to his right long enough to appraise the speaker, who turned out to be a short, pot-bellied man around his own age who was lounging up against a white picket fence. The street itself was otherwise deserted; quiet, refined and restful. So the whiskery fellow who stood before him now looked out-of-place, to say the least.

'Looking for something?' the man enquired.

He was wearing a crumpled black suit, red vest, white shirt and grey derby. And with his nose full of broken blood vessels and his skin as blotchy as skate, he looked to Sam like a whisky drummer who'd drunk all his stock and couldn't care less. His hazel eyes were bleary and bloodshot, his manner was unsteady, and his willingness to engage even a complete stranger in conversation were all classic symptoms of the long-time barfly.

'Lookin' for a boardin'-house run by a Mrs Brewer,' Sam replied.

The old rumpot's ruddy face creased into what was supposed to be a smile as he nodded. 'Ah, yes, I know it well. Look no further, my friend – you've arrived.' He indicated a large house two doors further along the street, a spacious place three storeys high, with clean windows, white lace curtains and ivy creeping like cancer up the cement-block walls.

'Obliged.'

'Welcome,' the smaller man responded, watching Sam step around him. 'Staying long?'

'No.'

'Shame. You look like an upright fellow. I'd like to have bought you a drink sometime.'

Sam let himself through a small gate in the fence and made his way along a sunflower-bordered path towards the boarding-house.

It was quite an impressive place, about the best in the whole street. Red roof tiles added a smart, colourful touch to the spot, as did the decorative stone mouldings set above the doors and windows.

Up on the porch he yanked at the bell-pull and waited, listening to the sound of hurried footsteps coming closer on the other side of the smoked-glass door. When it swung open, the middle-aged but nonetheless handsome woman in the lilac dress he'd seen getting her shopping at the general store earlier was revealed, wiping floury hands on a starched white apron.

'Yes?'

Sam set the cat down and swept off his Stetson. 'Mrs Brewer, is it?' he asked.

'Yes. What can I do for you?'

'I understand from Marshal Murphy that you rent out rooms by the day, week or month,' he said. 'I'd appreciate a bed for the night, if you've got one.'

Up close, Amelia Brewer was a lot more handsome than he'd first thought. The skin stretched across her high forehead, prominent cheekbones, long, straight nose and resolute chin looked soft and smooth. Her eyes were an interesting shade of gold, and her lips were full, pink and heart-shaped. The hair piled atop her regal head shone with a dozen different shades of red and copper. In all, she was quite a stunner.

By contrast, however, her appraisal of Sam was a little less than inspiring, and realising just how like a saddle-tramp he must look in his scuffed boots, russet-brown pants and out-of-vogue buckskin jacket, he couldn't really say that he blamed her.

'Just the night, Mr ... ah...?'

'Judge,' Sam supplied, reaching out to offer his hand. 'Sam Judge, town marshal from out of Austin Springs.'

Recognition passed across her face immediately. 'Why, I'm very pleased to meet you, marshal,' she replied, thawing somewhat. 'Come in, sir. I've read about you, often.'

She stepped back to allow him entrance.

The cat went in first, disappearing through a half-open door at the far end of the hallway.

'Oh–!'

'Pay her no mind, ma'am,' he said, running splayed fingers through his hair. 'She won't cause no trouble, honest.'

'If you say so,' the elegant landlady replied, not at all sure that such would be the case. 'I, ah, I don't usually allow my boarders to keep animals, but for such a celebrity…' Seeing his embarrassment, she tactfully changed the subject. 'I *do* have a room presently vacant. It's only small, but the bed is passable and the view of town is quite picturesque. The rent is two dollars and fifty cents per night, which includes an evening meal served promptly at six o'clock. All I ask of my boarders is that they refrain from drinking, swearing and using tobacco whilst under my roof. Oh, and of course, no wearing your boots in bed. Spurs do tear my linen so.'

Sam nodded agreeably. 'That sounds

admirable, ma'am.' He dug out some coins and placed them in her palm. When his fingertips touched her flesh a surprising – and awful pleasant – tingle washed through him.

'Come along,' she said, 'I'll show you up.'

He followed her up three flights of richly-carpeted stairs, fighting hard to keep his eyes off the movement of her shapely *derrière*. The house, he noted, was spotless, a haven of comfort in the wild blue mountains, full of knick-knacks, tintypes and Currier Ives prints.

'I hear that there was some sort of altercation in the centre of town earlier on,' she said conversationally. 'From what I heard from my neighbour Mrs Cunningham, I was very lucky to have missed it.'

He grunted.

'You seem to have come out of it un-scathed, however,' she went on, displaying a curious sense of pride. 'Proof positive that you really *are* as indestructible as *Beadle's Dime Library* would have us believe!'

At the head of the third and final flight of stairs, she turned to face him so suddenly that he nearly walked right into her. For one split second they were close enough for him to catch a noseful of the musky scent she favoured, and again he felt a strange tingle – although that might just have been the threat of a coming sneeze.

'I cannot tell you how many times I've read *Samuel Judge, The Pistol Prince,* marshal,' she confessed. 'How thrilling it must have been for you to have actually traded blows with Six-Knife Solomon and his band of cut-throats.'

'Yeah,' he replied distractedly. 'Thrillin'.'

She showed him into a small but comfortable room furnished with a strong brass bed, dresser, chair and wardrobe. Going in ahead of him, she hauled up the sash window to let some air in. Following her over, he spied the old rumpot still lounging against the white picket fence. Hearing the sound of the window being raised, the little man turned to offer them a smile and a wave.

Sam smiled. 'Who's the old drunk?' he asked.

'My husband,' she said.

She was halfway to the door before he reached out, touching her lightly on the arm. 'Hell... I mean heck... I'm sorry, ma'am. I didn't mean no disrespect, but it was a fool thing to say anyway. If you want me to leave–'

She turned back to face him, trying unsuccessfully to mask the pain on her face. 'No, no, that won't be necessary, marshal. I ... I'm quite aware of what Thomas is and...' With a supreme effort, she got herself under some sort of control. 'Please don't concern yourself any further,' she said formally. 'My husband and I are married in name only, marshal. A long time ago we elected to travel our own separate paths, me to build up this boarding establishment and he to fritter away the proceeds on Satan's hellish distillation.'

'I'm sorry to hear that, ma'am,' Sam mumbled, still angry with himself. 'You seem like a right fine woman, the type as shouldn't have to put up with such a burden – if you'll forgive me for sayin' so.'

She sniffed, lifted her apron to dab at her nose. 'We all have our cross to bear,' she said, keeping her eyes on the shining linoleum. 'Now, if you will excuse me…'

She turned and left the room hurriedly, closing the door behind her and leaving him to throw his saddle-bags on the bed and curse his own stupidity.

'Damn!'

With a sigh Sam peeled off his jacket, unbuckled his gunbelt, sat on the edge of the bed and hauled off his boots. He lay back on the fine feather mattress feeling tired as hell, but he knew he wouldn't sleep. It would take quite a while for his innards to calm down after the action of the afternoon, if past experience was anything to go by – and the image of Amelia Brewer's distraught face still lingered before his closed eyelids.

Ah hell…

He rolled onto his side. *I'm just four days from home,* he thought irritably, *and already I've captured one of the varmints I'm after.* He knew he should feel elated, but instead he just felt lousy.

He guessed there was just no pleasing some folk.

Somewhere along the line he must have dozed off, but the rest didn't do him much good; he woke up feeling even more bone-wary than he had before he'd closed his eyes. Sitting up again, he fingered his hair back off his forehead and stared out the window, contemplating roof upon roof scissoring away into the hazy distance, restless as all get-out.

Suddenly he thought of the letter he'd received on the day of the robbery. He still hadn't opened it. Well, now seemed as good a time as any. Getting to his feet, he crossed to his saddle-bags and delved inside. He had just closed his fingers around the long manilla envelope when he heard the sound of a gong being hammered downstairs.

Checking his pocket watch, he gave a low whistle. Six o'clock already; time for supper! Stuffing the envelope back into the saddle-bag, he hurriedly pulled his boots back on and straightened himself up in preparation for his next encounter with the beautiful Amelia.

Sam's fellow boarders – of whom there were six – were mostly clerks or book-keepers working up at the silver mines littering the north-eastern slopes of the mountains. They all joined Amelia and Thomas Brewer at a long table in a dining-room that boasted real back-East wallpaper and even a modest chandelier. They all knew who Sam was by this time, but wisely refrained from commenting on his reputation or the chaos he'd brought to Main Street earlier in the day.

Supper comprised a melt-in-the-mouth rabbit pie, boiled taters, greens and carrots, all of it washed down by good hot coffee, black and sweet, just how Sam favoured it.

Conversation was limited to one or two

complimentary remarks about the food and general speculation among the clerks as to who would strike the richest vein of silver this side of Thanksgiving. Sam, not feeling qualified to express an opinion, kept quiet and concentrated on enjoying his eats. Thomas Brewer, on the other hand, spoke loudly and incessantly on just about every subject. In a downtown saloon he would probably have been described as 'good company'. Here, in these otherwise genteel surroundings, however, he was little more than a pain in the ass.

To finish off, Mrs Brewer's part-time maid served up berry pie and cream. Everyone dug in until it was just a memory. Finally, when the meal was over and Amelia and the maid had started clearing the dishes, Thomas Brewer climbed unsteadily to his feet and announced his intention of strolling along to MacRory's, which to Sam sounded a lot like the name of a rough-and-ready drinking parlour.

While Sam refused an invitation to join

him, a couple of the clerks said that they quite fancied partaking of a cool glass of suds, and this they promptly went off to do. Soon Sam was left alone at the table, using a match to pick the food out of the gaps in his teeth. He grew so engrossed in the quest, in fact, that the next time Amelia appeared in the doorway, he jumped.

'Oh, Marshal Judge,' she said. 'Still here? I thought perhaps you might have repaired to the parlour by now or ... or joined my husband for his evening *jaunt*.'

Sam got to his feet, setting the match down hurriedly. 'No, ma'am. I was just settin' here, ah, gatherin' my thoughts, as they say. But if I'm in your way–'

'Not at all,' she replied, coming in to shut the door behind her. 'Pilar and I were all through here, anyway.'

From the general direction of the parlour next door came the sound of a tinny upright piano. Sam recognised a popular ballad entitled *There Will Never Be Another You, Mother.*

'That is Mr Weinberg,' Amelia Brewer explained with a smile, coming to sit across the table from him. 'He is quite good, don't you think?'

Sam nodded. 'Uh-huh.'

'I, ah, I meant to ask you, marshal...'

'Yes'm?'

'Did you find the "necessary" all right? I meant to point it out to you earlier, but in the, ah, the heat of the moment...'

'That's okay. Found it easy, ma'am.' In truth, not being used to such fancy indoor plumbing, he'd approached Mrs Brewer's dandified privy with more than a little trepidation, but after a couple of minutes he'd got used to it, and found it almost as comfortable as a real outdoor john.

'Ma'am—'

'Marshal—'

He smiled. 'Sorry,' he said. 'Go ahead.'

'Please, it was *I* who interrupted *you*,' she replied. 'You were saying?'

Sam sat down again, not particularly comfortable with the intimacy of their surroundings, but enjoying the pleasure of the woman's company all the same. 'Well, all I wanted to say really is that I'm sorry for … well, earlier on. I didn't mean to call your husband an old drunk–'

'Even if he is,' she said.

He shrugged. 'Well, whether he is or whether he ain't, it's not really for me to say. But I want you to know that whatever you told me this afternoon about you an' Mr Brewer, I've put it from my mind and won't ever tell another soul. My onliest hope now is that you'll forgive me my indiscretion.'

Once again, her smile chased the years from her face. 'I've already forgiven you, marshal. You weren't to know that Thomas was my husband, and in any case, you cannot be condemned for making what was a very honest observation.'

'Well … that's settled then,' he said.

'Yes,' she agreed. 'And yet I still sense something troubling you. Something to do with that outlaw you apprehended this afternoon, perhaps?'

'No,' he replied, then changed his mind and said, 'Yeah. Hell – sorry, ma'am – I don't really know. And anyway I shouldn't ought to palm all my problems off onto you.'

'Perhaps I am in the wrong,' she said. 'For prying into your personal affairs. But you know what they say about a problem shared, marshal.'

In the rich golden glow filtering down from the chandelier above, she looked beautiful and serene; so approachable, in fact, that something about her compelled him to break a lifelong rule and bitch aloud.

'Well, it's no secret, so I might as well tell you. I'm on the trail of some fellers robbed the Austin Springs bank. That was one of 'em I caught today. But...' He shook his head, unable to put his feelings into words. 'I figger I should feel mighty proud of myself right now, old-timer like me bringin' off an arrest like that. But instead I just feel so darn *lousy*, like *I'm* the villain of the piece.' He stared at her. 'Does that make any sense?'

Her face was a picture of concern. 'I don't know,' she replied, genuinely trying to understand what he was attempting to say. 'Did you feel the same way when you fought Six-Knife Solomon?'

To her surprise, he laughed. 'That was only a story, Mrs Brewer, just a pot-boiler dreamed up by that womanisin' jackanapes Eddie Judson.'

'Judson? Do you mean Mr Ned Buntline?'

'Buntline, Judson, he's all one and the same.'

She looked crestfallen. 'And all these years I believed every paragraph,' she said.

Seeing that he'd been wrong to burst her bubble, and feeling quite flattered that so fine a she-male should thrill to *his* alleged exploits, he sobered and said, 'Well, I *should* say it's a story-teller's way of recountin' events that actually took place.'

At once she brightened. 'Oh, I see! And have there been many such events in your life?'

He found himself warming to her attentions. 'Oh, hundreds,' he said modestly.

'Would you, I wonder...'

'Yes'm?'

'If I go fetch us some more coffee,' she said hesitantly, 'would you recount a few of them for me? Thomas won't be back until well after midnight, and the evenings get *so* lonely.'

He hid a grimace. 'Why, I'd be honoured, Mrs Brewer. If you're sure I won't bore you.'

'Oh, how could you?' she asked enthusiastically. 'Why, I have admired you for so many years, sir, the pleasure will be all mine!'

In later years he would look back upon that evening and find much to wonder about in two things; how he managed to find so many tall stories to tell her, and how she could be so gullible as to believe them all.

To hear him tell it, it was he who had fought off Santa Anna at the Alamo; he who hammered in the golden spike at Promontory, Utah; he who arm-wrestled Cochise for the hand of a beautiful Chiricahua princess; and he who tracked *loup-garou* through the swamplands of Louisiana with nothing more than a slingshot and daring.

If truth be known, however, Sam enjoyed himself almost as much as the woman, and was more disappointed than he'd thought possible when she rose at ten-fifteen to announce bedtime.

'But thank you, Marshal Judge. I cannot recall when an evening has been more scintillating, or the company so gallant.'

She offered her hand, and without thinking about it, no doubt emboldened by her kind words, he took it and pressed it to his lips. 'Thanks,' he replied. 'It's been swell, Mrs Brewer.'

They stared at each other, still holding hands, in the silent room, the silent house, his heart pounding even more than he felt sure hers must be.

Afterward, when he tried to recall who made the first approach, he really couldn't say for sure. But he had it in his mind that she called most, if not all, of the shots. Still, his memory of events grew hazy as the minutes ticked away, and he didn't think about much of anything during that first kiss, nor during the endless and hungry kisses that followed. He couldn't even remember puffing up three flights of stairs to his room, but they must've got there somehow.

'Amy,' he managed finally, disengaging himself from her embrace. 'I got to be honest with you – I don't b'lieve your husband would much appreciate what's goin' on up here!'

Through the darkness he heard her make a sound of disgust. 'My husband! I told you this afternoon, Samuel – Thomas and I are married in name only. Why, I seriously doubt that he would care whether I lived or died, so long as he had money enough to buy a drink!'

'Well,' Sam continued, punctuating his words with more feverish kisses, 'that's as maybe. But I'd purely hate for you to think I'd taken advantage of you in the mornin', sweet-thing, so it's best that you know up front that I'm ridin' out of here tomorrow, an' the next time I come back, it'll only be to collect a prisoner.'

'Yes … yes…'

'What I'm sayin' is,' Sam persisted, 'you mustn't read any more into this than there is…'

'What *is* there to read into it?' she asked, surprising him with her impatience. 'You are a man and I am a woman. Our … *appreciation* … of each other, I would hope, is mutual – as is our attraction. I want – and ask for nothing more than – one night with you, my hero!'

'You sure?' Sam asked worriedly.

'Mmmmfffmmfmfmff,' she replied.

They kissed again, passionately, until what was left of Sam's good ole Texas chivalry and resolve made him pull back one last time. 'Amy,' he said, shaking his head regretfully. 'I *really* don't think we should be doin' this.'

'Neither do I,' she replied honestly.

But what the hell – since it was only ten-thirty, and Thomas wasn't due home until gone midnight, they went ahead and did it anyway.

'Well,' Marshal Murphy said early next morning. 'What now? I told you Casey wouldn't change his mind. Not once he got it into his head that he had to pay for that little girl's murder.'

Sam nodded tiredly. 'That you did,' he agreed, stifling a yawn. Five minutes with the stubborn, death-set prisoner had made that abundantly clear. 'But fortunately, I ain't exactly run out of rope yet.'

He'd turned up at the law office just as the Long Branch lawman was finishing his ablutions. Now, ten minutes later, they were facing each other across Murphy's desk with Mitzi prowling around their feet like a miniature bobcat, pausing every so often to drink coffee from a saucer.

'Accordin' to my, ah, source of inform-ation back in Austin Springs,' Sam went on, 'them bank robbers had it in mind to cross the border an' head for a place called Linarez. Ever heard of it?'

'Can't say as I have,' Murphy said, lifting his own steaming mug.

'No matter. Guess I'll find out all there is to know about it soon enough.'

'You still think these *hombres*'re headed that way, then?' Murphy asked.

'Can't afford to think otherwise,' Sam pointed out. 'That's about the onliest clue I got to go on right now.'

'So you'll be leavin' this mornin'?'

'Right after I get me some breakfast,' Sam confirmed.

At the door a quarter-hour later, they shook hands one last time. 'Look after yourself, Judge,' Murphy said sincerely. 'I know we had, ah, *words*, yest'day when you first rode in. But I hope that's all water under the trestle now.'

'You can make book on it.'

Murphy smiled. 'Good. Your prisoner'll be waitin' for you safe 'n' sound next time you stop by.'

'Thanks.'

The bearded lawman's chocolate-brown eyes narrowed and his expression assumed a tone of embarrassment. 'Uh, one last thing, Judge...'

'Yeah?'

'Well ... don't take offence now, but... You sure you're, ah, up to this manhunt? It's just that you seem almighty stiff this mornin'. Might not be a good idea to go traipsin' off across these mountains if–'

'Stiff?' Sam repeated. Then the penny dropped. 'Oh. I, ah, I guess I just didn't sleep too good las' night.' Well, he told himself, it was no lie; Amelia Brewer'd had the same trouble. Briskly he clapped on his hat. 'But thanks for your concern, Murphy. Be seein' you soonest.'

As he shuffled off up the boardwalk, he was smiling; and thinking of the contented look on Amelia's beautiful face as they'd said their farewells thirty minutes earlier, feeling might proud of himself, too.

SIX

Sam was as good as his word. As soon as he'd finished wrapping himself around bacon, eggs and grits at a mid-town beanery and replenished his supplies in preparation for the coming journey, he saddled up old Charlie, set foot to stirrup and left Long Branch behind him. Soon only the high fastness of the Sangre de Christos towered around him.

During that first day it was easy to lose himself in the verdant shade of seemingly endless woodlands. Ponderosa and aspen kept him company for at least six or eight southbound miles. Much to his alarm, however, it appeared that the timber had grown eyes with which to watch his passage, although closer examination soon revealed that there were only peculiar stretch marks in the trees' light barks.

Relieved, he rode on, past the speckle-pod loco, holly-grape, blue columbine and ever-present sage that grew thick across the needle-littered forest floor.

As the miles unwound, so the character of the mountains changed. Green gave way to the greys and blues of misty, aeon-scarred canyons, gulches, arroyos and peaks. Here a stripe-tailed cacomistle darted from one rocky ledge to another; there a half-dozen wild horses crossed the hard-packed earth, searching for forage. The sky stayed practically cloudless, the weather clement, the air thin and debilitating.

But each mile Sam made was a mile closer to Linarez, and hopefully, a date with the remainder of the robbers.

Sometime around noon the following day, heavy rain-clouds began to bruise the sky. Then a strange, skin-stretching calm settled across the high country, and even the green jays, quetzals and plovers stopped filling the air with their birdsong and presence.

Knowing he had to find decent cover before the storm broke, Sam hauled back on the reins and quickly scoured the immediate vicinity for a likely spot. Eventually he found one at the foot of a steep, rocky slope; a large lip of sandstone projecting out over part of a wide, boulder-strewn clearing fringed with pine – but not before the initial deluge had soaked him right through to the skin.

Once they'd reached shelter, Sam dismounted and stood beside Charlie, watching the elements batter the mountains with their fury. The rain came down so hard that the pounding of it on his nature-formed roof deafened him whilst its sheer volume cut visibility to around five or six feet. Even Mitzi, who had hopped down from what, in the last week, had become *her* saddle-bag, seemed transfixed by the spectacle.

After a while, though, Sam grew uncomfortable enough in his sodden clothes to want to do something about it. Collecting dry wood from where it had fallen and gathered at the base of the hill, he prepared and lit a small fire. Then he off-saddled Charlie, ground-hobbled him too, and set about stripping down and drying off.

As he busied himself between fixing a pot of coffee and watching steam rise from his hat, jacket, shirt and undervest, his thoughts turned back to Austin Springs.

His First Street office, the Colorado State Bank, Katy Larrimer's eaterie, the stable on Erdoes Street ... he shook his head. Up here it was kind of hard to remember that they still existed. Likewise with Jack O'Neal, Heck Mabey, Wallace Corey, Len Meares...

He shook out and pulled on his spare clothes – a bone-coloured nankeen shirt, grey pants (part of a Sunday-go-to-meeting suit he'd once owned) and black waistcoat. Immediately he felt more comfortable.

Somehow his perspective had been narrowed, blinkered by all those years spent growing old in Austin Springs. He'd become stuck in his ways, apt to forget that there was a world beyond the confines of the town that was not *quite* as civilised as it would like to believe. A world where men could still be men.

The pot on the fire began to bubble. He poured a mug of coffee, stirred in some sweetening and blew on it to cool it. Nearby Mitzi rooted through some loose rocks to see what she could turn up. When the lawman sneezed, she arched her back, startled.

Sam was seven days out of Austin Springs now, and according to the map in George Murphy's office, about two days from Linarez. Blowing his nose on a none-too-clean square of rag, he wondered what still lay ahead for him – and how he would feel when his manhunt was over.

Still, any such speculation was kind of academic right now. After all, he might stop a bullet before he could round up Baylor Ryan and his cronies, in which case *nothing* would matter anymore.

But what if he *did* pull it off? How easy would it be for him to settle down again now that he'd discovered – or rather, *re-*discovered – the lift that suited him best?

It would be tough, for sure, he thought. Mayhaps even impossible.

As he recalled how vital he'd felt in the past week, the word *exhilaration* came into his mind. He'd read it in a newspaper one time, and thinking it was some sort of cuss-word he'd never heard before, looked it up in a dictionary. What it actually meant was 'to enliven or animate'.

But he didn't feel all that lively right now. In fact, he felt downright lousy; tired and stiff, achy and short-tempered. Still, that was to be expected. Thin mountain air did that to a body after a while, just like old age.

He shivered.

As the afternoon wore on, Sam grew more and more stiff-limbed and sneezy. The rain eased up a little; soon it settled down to a steady drizzle. But feeling more than a tad lack-lustre by then, he decided to stay beneath the protection of the sandstone lip for the rest of the day.

When darkness finally came, it found him sprawled by the dying fire, asleep and breathing raggedly. Mitzi came over, gave him an experimental sniff, then padded away, mystified. Her master felt hot, looked red, was slick with sweat.

And as his chest rumbled with the effort of breathing, his lips twitched in an endless litany of silent, desperate mutterings.

Mitzi's sharp cry echoed across the boulder-strewn clearing and brought him up from beneath his blanket. For a moment he wasn't sure where he was. The land around him was dark and silent. To the west the tall pines rose skyward, stretching out into a shapeless black mass. Overhead was the sandstone shelf. Beside him sat a bed of shifting embers.

Then he had it. The rain. He'd been soaked. He peered into the night; it had stopped now. Moonlight bounced off wet rocks and splashed its full white face in a dozen puddles. In the distance he picked out a faint but regular *drip-drip-drip* coming from the pines; the last of the rainwater falling from the branches.

Shivering, he turned his head and spoke the fat Abyssinian's name.

The only reply, however, was a low, throaty chuckle that came from behind him.

Quickly he twisted back the other way; froze. Four men were standing about seven or eight feet away. He could just about make out their night-cloaked shapes. They had handguns drawn and aimed his way.

'Wha–?'

When they took a step forward, into the dull ember-glow, he narrowed his eyes. Four men. Four men coming into the light. Vaguely familiar.

He recognised them now.

'*Don't move!*' It was Baylor Ryan who spoke the command, holding his Colt's Peacemaker steady on the lawman's thin face.

Sam was too shocked to move anyway. Slowly he ran his still-bleary eyes across each of their fire-reddened faces. Ryan; Sadillo; Hayes; Dalton. His heart sank. Somehow they'd found out he was after them. How?

Matt? Had he managed to contact them, tip them off? If so, why? Just whose side was he on?

Sam released his breath in a shallow sigh. Of only one thing was he certain right now – that his quarry had doubled back to bring the showdown to *him*.

Damn. He should've considered that possibility, planned for it. Now he felt sick at having been caught so flat-flooted. If only he'd been more *cautious*...

But there was no more time for recriminations. Not if he wanted to stay alive. As the last clouds of sleep left his mind, he realised that he was still wearing his gunbelt. And his right hand was still hidden beneath his blanket. That was something, he guessed.

It was a slim enough chance, though; nothing to get excited about. In order to beat those buckos, he'd have to roll, thumb forward the Remington's retaining thong, haul iron – and out-shoot the *four* of them.

From where he sat, it looked like a mighty tall order, even for the man Ned Buntline's once called 'The Pistol Prince'.

Then Sadillo opened his mouth to speak, his words breaking in on Sam's thoughts. 'You should'n oughta've come after us, Judge,' he chastised mildly. 'You' gonna have to pay for that.'

'Yeah,' said Hayes. And before Sam could rise up and tell them to go to hell, the slab-shouldered Negro lifted his left hand, in which he held the limp, throat-cut body of—

'*Mitzi!*'

The cat's name echoed around the chilly overhang, but Sam heard it only as an expression of grief; nothing more distinguishable than that.

Then everything jumped into sharp focus. The Mexican laughed at him. They all did. He realised that they were going to play with him before they killed him. He was going to *amuse* them. Be their *sport*.

Or so they thought.

Somehow he managed to tear his stinging eyes away from the dead cat and look directly into the heat-flushed faces of his captors. It was in that moment that he coolly and calmly decided that he was going to change the rules a little, so that they would find themselves playing *his* game.

A game called *Kill Or Be Killed*.

With a bellow of defiance, his right hand moved beneath the coarse grey blanket, grabbing for the Remington. But even as his fingertips touched the worn, cross-hatched grips, he knew he was too late. Four guns roared, waking echoes; four bullets ripped through the blanket; four holes opened in his chest; four jets of steaming blood erupted to land sizzling in the fire–

He woke up.

'Wha … whaddisit … What…?'

Silence.

Sam looked around. From the colour of the sky and the position of the sun, he figured it was just about dawn. Although it was still chilly, he was drenched with sweat. He felt heavy-headed, almost unable to move for the stiffness in his limbs. But somehow he managed to lift his head, peer down at his chest.

No bullet holes. No blood.

Clearing his throat, he called Mitzi's name softly.

After a moment the cat wandered out of the shadows at the back of the overhang to offer him another sniff. The coldness of her small button nose was welcome against his feverish cheek.

'A dream,' he said. Or *thought* he said. But it had all been so *vivid*.

He closed his eyes again, knowing that something was wrong with him but unable to pinpoint exactly what it was. He felt awful. His head ached. His chest felt clogged. He was burning up and giddy as hell.

Then he recalled the stiffness George Murphy had commented on the day he'd left Long Branch, and the drenching he'd taken just before he'd found this sheltered spot. He groaned. *The grippe,* he realised despondently. *I reckon I got the grippe.*

Ah hell – of all the times to fall ill…

Still, there wasn't much he could do about it now except let it run its course. He hated to lose time over it, but he didn't really see that he had much option. It was all he could do to try and sit up. Riding a horse would be damn' nigh impossible.

With streaming eyes and runny nose, he lay back down and pulled his blanket right up to his stubbly chin, seeing no alternative but to try and sleep the fever away.

Linarez, New Mexico; seventeen hours later.

'Gentlemen,' Jeremiah Curry had announced at seven o'clock, 'the name of the game is poker. No musers, no leaders and bleeders, and no hole cards wired to a straight. Just pure, unadulterated five-card stud. You in?'

The other four men seated at the baize-topped table in the poorly-lit back room of the Cup Floweth Over Saloon had nodded or mumbled their assent.

'Right.'

And that was how it had started.

Now, four hours later, the last hand was about to be played.

Curry was an elegant-looking man some-where in his thirties, with a clear, ruddy face, curly brown hair, bemused blue eyes and a most unnerving smile. As far as the other players had been able to judge from his mode of dress – black frock-coat, tailored grey pants, ruffled white shirt and shiny silk vest – he was a professional gambler. Furthermore, his diamond stick-pin, $600 Jurgensen pocket watch and the veritable mountain of paper money stacked neatly before him pegged him as a gent who won more often than he lost.

In a way he seemed curiously out of place here in the saloon's dingy back room, sipping Kentucky bourbon from a smudged glass. But Jim Dalton and Lester Hayes, who had bought into the game at seven, both knew why he put up with the sur-roundings.

It was because there was no law in

Linarez, unless you counted the part-time peacekeeper who left his ailing farm once a month to get into town for the day. Curry was free to fleece the marks as many times as he liked without fear of prosecution.

Still, they could hardly condemn him for that. The Austin Springs bank robbers had come to town for pretty much the same reason.

Not that Linarez was a hell-town, exactly. Too many honest folks still outnumbered the *dis*honest ones for that. But the 'knavish' element was tolerated, even *encouraged* if they had money in their pockets that was just aching to be spent, as long as they kept to themselves and made no trouble for anyone else. In a predominantly dry land where the raising of crops and livestock often proved impossible, they were good for local business. What you might call a necessary evil.

Baylor, Raul, Lester and Jim had ridden in about four days earlier and promptly set themselves up in a joy-house on the east side of town. Once Baylor had found a doctor to dig Art Casey's slug out of his shoulder, the four young guns had set about enjoying their wealth – with a vengeance.

After the rigours of their mountain crossing, Jim guessed they'd gone a little crazy. Champagne, women, cards and dice; it had been ninety-six hours of virtually non-stop debauchery.

And why not? They had the money to pay for it. And since it was Linarez' proud boast that no lawman, be he U.S. Marshal, Pinkerton detective or representative of the Army, had ever dared to come and serve a wanted paper on anyone staying in town, it seemed safe to relax and enjoy themselves.

But tonight the good life was beginning to pall, at least as far as Jim Dalton was concerned. While Baylor and Raul seemed happy enough to drink themselves silly out front of the saloon, Jim, Les and a couple of townies decided to accept Jeremiah Curry's invitation to a private poker game being held out back. At the time it had sounded like fun, a change from boozing and whoring, a new experience – playing against a professional cardsharp.

Too bad things had only gone from bad to worse.

Jim had started the game with three thousand dollars. Now, with the time at just a couple of minutes before eleven o'clock, he'd been forced to sell his prized Spanish colonial spurs to the fellow next to him, a retired Western Union manager who'd taken quite a shine to them, just to raise a big enough stake for this last game.

Seated on the other side of Dalton, Lester Hayes, who had only dropped two hundred dollars during the course of the evening, watched Curry shuffle the deck. There was no cheating going on that he could see; hadn't been all night. Curry had produced a sealed pack of Climax playing cards at the start of the session, proving that the deck was in no way marked. And if he was pulling aces and kings from anyplace else, then he was a magician, for the quiet Negro hadn't caught a single untoward movement of his long, dextrous fingers.

But he could sense Jim growing more and more agitated beside him, and glanced worriedly at his friend's sharp profile. Dalton's black, glittering eyes were fixed on Curry's hands as the tinhorn shuffled the deck, offered them to the Western Union man to cut and shuffled again. Dalton ran his fingers through his thick black hair and reached for the cigarette smoking away on the table's edge. His long, narrow face was white and sweaty, his eyes looped by weary grey half-circles.

Lester didn't know what'd gotten into him. He'd been playing like a madman all night; bluffing even when he held a lousy hand, drawing to inside straights and making little attempt to mask his emotions. The Negro didn't want to think how Jim'd react if he lost this last game.

Curry dealt the cards with practiced ease, stopping when a small pile lay before each of the players. Without a word, the men picked up their hands, fanned them out and took their first look of the game. All of them, with the exception of Curry, who looked just as fresh as a daisy, were beginning to show signs of exhaustion now. Shirts were sticking to hot flesh, sweat-stains darkened armpits and spines. It was difficult to focus on the numbers and suits of the cards. But no-one complained.

It was very quiet in the smoke-and-shadow-filled room. Even the sounds of merriment coming through the thin wooden door behind Curry seemed muted.

'I'll open for twenty,' said the Western Union man. He placed a couple of ten-dollar bills in the centre of the table, which the others then matched.

Silence fell across the table again. Curry set his cards face down on the baize and took a drink from the glass beside his stake money.

'Cost you thirty to stay in,' replied the fifth man, a railroad engineer from Mammoth, Arizona.

A nerve in Dalton's cheek twitched. His black eyes shuttled from the cards clenched in front of him to the other four players. 'Cost you...' He swallowed. 'Cost you fifty,' he said.

Curry eyed him closely, then glanced around the table. Finally, he dug five tens from his pile and tossed them into the pot. One by one each of the others ante'd up. Then Curry picked up what remained of the deck and looked enquiringly at the Western Union man.

'Two,' the elderly fellow said in reply to his unspoken question. He threw the two cards he didn't want into the centre of the table, making sure they remained face down. Curry then dealt out his replacements.

Dalton asked for one. Hayes took two. The railroader passed, saying, 'I'm fine as I am.' Curry took one.

The five men examined their hands again, each of them ignoring the music and laughter echoing around outside. Dalton wet his lips. The railroad man scratched his bushy beard. Hayes reached for his glass and took a drink.

'Cost you a hundred to stay in,' the Western Union man said at last, throwing some bills into the pot.

The railroader stared at him a moment, then threw his hand in. 'Too rich for me.' He sat back and took a sip from his beer glass. Some of the suds stuck to his moustache.

Curry shrugged and ante'd up without speaking. So did Hayes.

'See your hundred,' said Dalton. 'An' raise you a hundred.'

All eyes turned to the sharp-faced youngster as he threw the last of his money – the last of his share from the Austin Springs bank job – into the centre of the table.

'Sounds like you mean business,' Curry remarked easily.

'I do.'

The remaining players put their money into the pot. A quick mental tally told Hayes that it now contained about eleven hundred and fifty dollars; not even half of what Jim had brought to the game with him, but better than nothing, he guessed.

If he could win it, that was.

The air around the table was thick with tension as Curry said, 'All right, gentlemen – let's see what you've got.'

Hayes, who figured he had a pretty good hand, set down the three, four and eight of hearts, the eight of diamonds and the eight of spades. He ran his brown eyes around the table, searching for reactions, his own flat face expressionless.

The Western Union man threw in a losing hand. 'Can't beat that, I'm afeared.'

Dalton sucked in his breath. He'd gone so pale that Hayes thought he was going to throw up. But then the black-eyed bank robber set down four sevens and the ten of spades.

'I … I win,' he mumbled as if he couldn't believe his luck.

'I don't think so,' Curry replied with that unnerving smile twisting his lips. He turned

over his cards, revealing the king of diamonds – and four aces.

Hayes stared at the hand with surprise and
admiration. *'Judas!'*

But Curry's only reaction was an easy
chuckle. 'Seems to have been my lucky
night,' he said in understatement. He had
just set about collecting his winnings when
he glanced up at Dalton, whose words had
been lost beneath the scraping of his chair-
legs. 'I'm sorry. Did you say something, my
friend?'

Dalton cleared his throat. 'Yeah. An' I ain't
your friend.'

The bank robber's angry tone made the
other men freeze in the act of rising from
their seats. Curry, however, only smiled,
doubtless trying to defuse a possibly trouble-
some situation.

'Well, would you care to say it again,
then?' he invited pleasantly. 'Only this time
a little louder?'

Dalton nodded. 'I called you a cheat,' he
said in a strangled voice.

'Jim…'

'Butt out, Les! This is 'tween me 'n' him!'

The Western Union man swallowed nervously as Curry rose slowly to his feet. He, the railroader and Hayes all backed off to allow the two adversaries to face each other squarely across the table.

But while Dalton's right hand hovered dangerously close to the grips of his ancient Dance Brothers Army .44, Curry made no move to defend himself. Indeed, so far as they could see, he wasn't even armed.

'Is that what the rest of you think as well?' Curry asked quietly, turning from the Western Union man and the railroader to Hayes. 'That I've been cheating you?'

Hayes shook his head. 'Nope. Ah reckon you been playin' it square all night.'

Dalton looked at his friend in amazement. 'Huh? He comes up with all the aces an' you say he didn't cheat? What's the matter wi' you, Les, you stupid? Come on, Curry, off with that jacket! Let's see just how you're wired up under those fancy sleeves!'

'Now see here–'

'Jim–'

'Damn you, then–'

Suddenly chaos broke out as Dalton went for his gun. As the Western Union man and the railroader back-pedalled to hug the wall, Curry dropped out of sight beneath the table.

Dalton's bullet tore through the flimsy door behind the gambler. In an instant yells and screams replaced the laughter outside. Under the table, Curry hurriedly produced a Derringer. Another gunshot sounded as the .41 calibre bullet ripped up through the baize-topped table and ploughed into the ceiling, showering Dalton with plaster.

'Jim!'

But Hayes' cry fell on deaf ears. Lowering his aim, Dalton fired another shot. A second hole appeared in the table-top. The cards jumped, the railroader's beer glass fell to the floor and smashed. Curry cried out although he hadn't been hit.

Suddenly the door behind the tinhorn

flew open, slamming back into the wall with a thundery crash. In the frame stood a great big man with a sawn-down Purdey shotgun in his hands. As he raised the weapon Hayes and Dalton recognised him as Slick Harry Miles, the saloon's resident bouncer.

Hayes' eyes saucered in horror as he yelled, *'Don't shoot!'*

But when it came to an outbreak of gun-play in *his* saloon, Miles didn't wait to listen to reason. Already his thick right index finger was tightening on the Purdey's trigger. As it exploded, sending a diamond pattern of .00 buckshot their way, Hayes and Dalton hit the floorboards, moment-arily deafened by the detonation.

The lead balls made a mess of the wall before which they'd just been standing, but did no more damage than that. As Slick Harry broke open the shotgun and reached for fresh rounds, Hayes came up into a crouch.

'No mo,' Slick Harry! We surrender!'

But Jeremiah Curry, still hiding under the

table, had other ideas. 'Shoot them, man! They're armed!'

And Dalton was just as hungry for blood himself. As he rose back up to his full height, his formerly-pasty face was bright crimson and twisted in fury. 'Try to blast me, would you!'

He raised his gun again, this time intent on hitting Slick Harry, who was a bald-headed giant with the kind of face only a blind mother could love.

Fearing the worst, a saloon girl behind the bouncer screamed. But before Dalton could retaliate, Hayes took the initiative. Lashing out with his meaty right fist, he caught his friend on the jaw with a hard, tooth-loosening cross. Dalton's black eyes rolled up into his head and he dropped his gun to the floor. With a moan his legs went out from under him and he promptly collapsed on top of it.

'Ah tellin' you, Slick Harry – no mo' shootin'!'

At that moment, Baylor and Raul pushed

through the crowd behind them to join Slick Harry in the doorway. Their faces were still flushed with booze, but it looked as if they were sobering up fast. 'Just what the hell's been happenin' here?' Baylor demanded angrily. He was still wearing his tight leather gloves, even on the hand that was dangling from the sling around his neck.

'Long story,' sighed Hayes.

'Can we go before you start tellin' it?' the Western Union man asked anxiously.

Hayes shrugged. 'Ah guess, lessen Harry here's got any objections.'

The bouncer, having calmed down a bit, glanced around the room. 'Not a one,' he grunted. 'Plain enough to see they di'n't start this ruckus.'

While he was in a forgiving mood, Baylor told him, 'We'll pay for the damages, Harry – providin' Lester an' Jim was to blame.'

'We was,' said Hayes, throwing a look at the unconscious Dalton. 'Leastways, Jim was.'

'All right,' growled Harry. 'Let's hear it.'

175

Hayes was just about to comply when he called the Western Union man's name. 'Befo' you go, Ah got a question for you.'

The retired manager looked very pale. 'Me? S – sure, anything,' he replied nervously.

'C'n I buy Jim's spurs back offen you? Ah'll give you fifty dollars for 'em; that's ten bucks more'n you paid. It's jus' that I got a feelin' Ah'm gonna have to do somethin' real nice to make the peace 'tween us when he come roun' agin.'

SEVEN

The following dawn Sam opened his still-watery eyes and slowly moved his head to scan his immediate surroundings. The high country morning was quiet save for the birdsong that came from the nearby pines, and peaceful. Some little distance away,

Charlie had his head bent and was chewing grass. Just behind him, a big red squirrel busied itself unearthing stored nuts.

It was still too early to say, of course, but the ageing lawman felt that the worst of his 'flu was over. Well, if his growling stomach was anything to go by, his appetite had come back anyway, and he took that to be a good sign. There was just one problem – his ribs. They still felt as tight as a matron's corset.

'…uh…'

With an effort he raised his head to peer down at his blanket-draped torso. That was when he saw Mitzi hunched protectively on his chest and cracked his first smile in days.

'Well I'll be damned,' he muttered, clearing his throat. 'Go on, get offa me, you crazy cat.' The Abyssinian did so, fast, and the pressure on his ribs vanished at once. 'No wonder I could hardly get my breath!'

Slowly he sat up and stretched. So far so good. His pocket watch had stopped, but by the position of the sun he estimated it to be somewhere around six, six-thirty.

As soon as he made it to his feet he knew he was on the mend. All he could recall of the previous day was an endless round of sleeping, dreaming and waking. But now he felt much more alert; almost like his old self again.

Still, he knew better than to run before he could walk, and if he was honest with himself, he still felt kind of woozy. So he took his time about building a fire and boiling some coffee, and then pulled a can of apple slices from his saddle-bags just to settle his stomach.

He took his ease like that for the rest of the day, still coughing and wheezing every so often, and sleeping whenever his eyelids drooped, but content in the knowledge that at least he was getting better.

Next morning he felt ready and anxious to ride. He still wasn't a hundred percent, but from now on he figured to recuperate whilst on the move.

He saw no other human being for the

remainder of his trek across the mountains, and precious little in the way of wildlife, either. The peaks were harsh and rugged now, too barren even for the animals. But at least the weather remained fine, and there were no more storms.

Finally, as his strength returned and he found himself able to smoke his noxious cigars without choking again, the land began to dip. It grew hot as he reached the south-eastern foothills, but that didn't bother him; to the contrary, it helped him sweat the last of the fever out of his bones.

At some time during that third day he guessed he must have crossed the border, for New Mexico's dry, uneven and largely desert-like terrain began to make itself known all around him. He consulted the tiny map he'd been carrying around inside his head and was pleased with what he saw there. He wasn't far from Linarez now; as much as anything else, he could *feel* it.

With anticipation lighting his gaze, he kept the roan pointed south-east.

Sometime around mid-morning he picked up and followed a wagon trace trending south, and at three o'clock that afternoon, got his first glimpse of the town.

Set against a backdrop of gentle, mesquite-dotted hills, it looked just like any other middle-sized wilderness community; a scattering of maybe two hundred-odd adobe and timber buildings spreading out from a central, ornate stone well, with wide streets and regular, although light, wagon and horseback traffic.

Sam entered Main Street at a walk, on his guard and with eyes everywhere. Fortunately, however, his arrival stirred little interest. His was just one more passing face.

Every building, it seemed, had a shingle proclaiming its purpose. Restaurants and club rooms shared street-space with boot stores, sign works and drugstores. Here was the office of a real-estate broker, there a tiny wooden cabin that offered washing and ironing at cheap rates. He saw a post office and bakery, a few saloons and a liquor store – but nowhere did he see the headquarters of the local law.

Dismounting, he stopped a woman wheeling a sleeping baby in a tassel-topped carriage and asked directions to the marshal's office. She was a pretty woman with hazel eyes and reddish-brown hair, and for a moment he was reminded of Amelia Brewer. Then the woman told him that there was little point in sending him right the way across town because the part-time constable, Jeb Ross, wasn't due in from his farm fifteen miles away until the July Fourth parade, which was being held in three days' time.

Sam suddenly realised the significance of all the flags and banners he'd seen flapping in the cooling breeze. 'A July Fourth parade?' he echoed. ''Scuse me, ma'am, but do you mean to tell me that today is the first of July?'

She gave him a strange look. 'Why, yes.'

He nodded slowly and touched his hat.

'Thanks, ma'am. You been real kind.' As he watched her wheel the carriage away, he smiled to himself, then turned back to his horse and remounted. 'Well, fellers, what do you know?' he asked, addressing the roan and the cat, whose big tan head as just visible beneath the flap of his right-hand saddle-bag. 'It's my birthday.'

He was forty-six years old.

Joining the flow of traffic that seemed to be leading into the commercial district, he digested what the young mother had told him. A part-time 'constable' who spent most of his time planting crops fifteen miles away? No wonder Ryan and his buddies had made a beeline for Linarez.

Tying Charlie to the hitch-rack outside a passably clean-looking restaurant, he loosened his cinch and told Mitzi not to leave the safety of her saddle-bag. Then he went inside, found a table by the curtained window and ordered liver and bacon, mashed potatoes, onions and coffee.

It was as he paid the tab that he began

what was to be a long afternoon of questioning. Had the waitress or her boss seen the 'friends' he was after? They didn't think so. He described them in some detail, but the answer was still sorry, no.

Emerging back out onto the street, he re-buckled his saddle, climbed aboard and kept riding until he found a stable. There he paid for a night's board for his horse and asked the livery-hand if *he'd* seen the 'friends' Sam was after.

'No sir, I'm afraid I ain't.'

'Not to worry,' Sam sighed. 'Be safe to leave all my saddle-gear here, will it? Includin' the cat?'

'Sure.'

'Thanks.'

But outside he allowed himself a mental curse. There had to be better ways of finding needles in haystacks – always assuming, of course, that the needles *he* was looking for were still here for the finding. With a sigh he turned left. For the time being, at least, it seemed that he had no alternative but to keep asking around until something turned up.

So he enquired after his elusive 'friends' down at the Rock Bottom Saloon, the Copper Pot Saloon, the Yellow Flower and the Bull's Head. In desperation he even tried the Idle Hour Men's Club Room and the office of the Linarez *Tribune*, which was just next door. But in every one he came up empty.

Around eight o'clock that night he wandered tiredly into the Cup Floweth Over on Loughlin Street. By then he was sick of saloons, and had decided that this was positively the last one he was going to try his luck in tonight.

Bellying up to the bar, he ordered a beer and stood there eyeing the other patrons over the rim of his glass. The warm yellow glow of a dozen kerosene lamps illuminated only the usual mix of townies and passing tradesmen he had come to know so well. Glumly he ordered another beer, then asked the blond bartender about his 'friends'.

The bartender smiled and said, 'Oh, *them.*'

Across the counter, Sam stiffened. 'They've been in here?' he asked sharply.

The bartender nodded. He was a youngish man, dressed in a cool white shirt, black vest and green, pull-on protective sleeves. 'And *how!*' he replied. 'Darn near shot this place to pieces about two, three nights ago. Well, leastways two of 'em did. The black feller and the one with the fancy spurs.'

Sam swallowed, struggling to stay calm. 'Oh,' he said casually. 'That'd be, ah, Les an' Jim.'

'If you say so. I didn't catch their names.'

'What happened, then?'

In a few short sentences, the bartender recounted the events of Jim Dalton's ill-fated card game. But when Sam asked him where 'the boys' were staying, he could only shrug and say, 'Sorry, I don't know.'

Sam nodded, trying to appear uncon-cerned even though his blood was pound-ing. 'Don't matter. I daresay I'll run into 'em soon enough – unless they've already quit town.'

'Sure. Linarez is only so big. But I reckon they'll stick around for the July Fourth parade, don't you?'

'Maybe.'

'Anyway, you could always ask Mr Curry, I guess.'

'Curry?'

'The gambler said spur-wearing gent took a couple shots at. He ain't in tonight; ain't been in since it happened, in fact. But you can probably find him at his hotel, the New-man, on Hammer Street. He could likely tell you where to find 'em.'

Sam pushed away from the bar, leaving his second beer untouched. 'Thanks, friend. I'm beholden.'

When Sam went back out into the darkness he was in high spirits. Getting directions from the first person he came to, he headed for the Newman Hotel. A seven-minute walk brought him to his destination. A five-dollar bill slipped across the counter to the night-clerk got him Jeremiah Curry's room number. And a climb up thirty-four carpeted stairs finally got him to the room itself.

He knocked, once. A guarded voice asked who was there. Sam didn't bother telling him. Lifting his right foot, he kicked the door open and followed it into a very pleasant and well-lit apartment.

Curry was lying on a double bed. He was in his shirt-sleeves and there was a newspaper in his hands. He looked terrified when Sam kicked the door shut behind him.

'What ... what...'

As impressions of cold-water fish went, his was pretty good. But Sam told him to calm down before he did himself a mischief, then produced two five-dollar bills, part of the savings he kept in a box under the floorboards back in his office, and tossed them to the dandified gambler.

'Feller tried to punch your ticket the other night,' he said.

Fearing the worst, Curry's eyes bugged.

'You … he sent you to…'

'No, he didn't. Now, pick up the money; it's to pay for the damage I just did to your lock.'

Curry stopped quaking and glanced down at the crumpled bills. Warily he asked, 'What … uh- … what is it that you want, exactly?'

'I want to know where I can find him.'

Thirty seconds later he had his answer – and it was just about the best damn' birthday present he'd ever had.

Lily Clubb's Parlour of Fun was a square, two-storey building constructed from red bricks and black slates. It stood alone among a series of empty lots on the east side of town, a rather grand structure set in what, judging from the various signs of construction Sam had seen on his way there, would one day become a very select neighbourhood.

The joy-house was ablaze with light now, a beacon shining through the night, inviting red-blooded males everywhere to come ahead an' don't be shy – providing they could afford it.

Sam was standing across the street from it, his eyes moving from one velvet-smothered window to another as he listened to the sounds of revelry coming from within. It sounded to him like they had an entire orchestra in there, but it was more likely a string quartet. Absently he tapped his foot to the rhythm of a lively Viennese waltz as he decided on a plan of action.

He couldn't just burst in there now; there'd be too many innocent bystanders in the way. And neither did he fancy spending the rest of the night waiting for everyone to go to bed – to *sleep*, that was – before attempting a break-in.

Problems, problems...

Whichever way he viewed it, his best bet was to hit the place at first light, catch his adversaries with their pants down. Literally.

He chuckled.

First light, then. For the *last* showdown.

It sounded good.

It had long been the custom of Miss Clubb's girls – and of Miss Clubb herself, for that matter – to sleep late in the mornings. Which, considering the unsociable hours they usually kept, was only to be expected. So when the bell at the front of the house jangled at 6:30 a.m., only Ellery, the doorman, Mabel, Miss Clubb's cook and Josephine, her personal maid, were up and about, breakfasting in the big, sunshiny kitchen out back.

As Ellery rose and slowly made his way through the sleeping house, a steady stream of invective spilled from his thin, pinched lips. He was a sixty-year-old Negro from Enterprise, Alabama, tall but stooped now, with loose legs, long arms, tight white hair and rheumy eyes. He had been Miss Clubb's doorman for the last eight years, four here and four down in Hereford, Texas. He was happy with his duties, content with his often generous tips, and he enjoyed the seniority he had over the rest of the servants.

But he did not like having his bacon and toast interrupted at six-thirty in the morning. Not by anyone.

I mean, he asked himself as he picked his way around the discarded bottles, glasses, garters and shoes left over from last night's roistering, who the heck would come a-calling at this hour, anyway? Didn't they know that life in the Parlour of Fun never started 'til six o'clock in the *evening?*

Reaching the wide front door, Ellery ran his dark hands briskly down his white shirt, brushing away a scattering of breakfast crumbs and smoothing the cotton to look presentable. Then he pulled back the bolts, released the chain, twisted the door handle and peered out.

The barrel of a Remington Army .44 stared him in the face.

'Open up,' Sam growled in a low whisper. *'Now.'*

With the look of shock still frozen onto his face, Ellery lifted his hands and backed up a step. Sam came in and pushed the door shut behind him. Glancing around, he found himself in an ostentatious reception area with paintings of big-busted she-males on the walls and inch-thick carpet underfoot.

'Four men,' he told the startled doorman. 'I know they're lodgin' here. I want to know which rooms they're in.'

Ellery stumbled and stuttered for a second or two. 'L-lot o' menfolks stayin' h – heah,' he pointed out.

'You'd know these four,' Sam said tightly, keeping the Remington jammed into the other man's face. 'One's got red hair and freckles, wears black gloves all the time. Second one's a little Mexican, pock-marked face, moustache, fancy woolly chaps. Third one's a black feller like yourself, only bigger, heavier, around twenty-two, twenty-three; and the fourth's a weasel-faced youngster, wears hard-to-miss spurs on his Justins.'

Recognition passed across Ellery's sweat-damp face. He knew the men Sam was talking about, all right. But he didn't reply directly. 'You … you the law?' he asked.

Sam nodded. 'I *represent* the law.'

'Show me yo' badge.'

With his left hand, he pulled aside his buckskin jacket to reveal the star on his nankeen shirt. Before Ellery could look at it closely, however, he let the jacket fall back to cover it. 'Now,' he said. 'Where are they?'

The doorman's eyes flickered upwards. 'F...first four rooms you come to at ... at the top o' the stairs.'

Sam fixed him with a hard stare until he was convinced that Ellery was telling it true. 'Right. Now – go back to your room and stay there, and you won't get hurt. Make sure the rest of the servants do the same. And don't do anything foolish, mister. There's bone orchards all over that's just full to burstin' with fellers as tried to play the hero.'

'B...but jus' you hold up, you lawman. This heah's a respect'ble–'

'Save it.'

'We don't want no gunplay in h–'

Sam wheeled on him. *'Just do what I told you!'*

Backing away, Ellery turned and disappeared through the door to the servants' quarters while Sam passed through a curtained alcove and into a large, opulent room furnished with chairs, sofas and fancy occasional tables. Along the wall to his right was a polished mahogany bar and enough liquor to sink a ship. Opposite stood a raised platform which no doubt housed the quartet when they were playing.

The item he was looking for – the winding staircase – began directly to his left. Still holding the handgun firm, he began to ascend, as quiet as fog.

That's it, he told himself, *nice 'n' calm...*

He was halfway upstairs when Ellery returned from out back clutching a Henry repeater. *'Ever'-body watch out up there! We' bein' raided!'*

With a curse Sam spun just as the elderly doorman fired the rifle at him. Immediately he dropped low, but there was no need. The .44 calibre bullet went wide, slapping into a landscape on the wall about fifteen feet below him.

Still, the damage had already been done.

Even as Ellery jacked another shell into the Henry, Sam became aware of high, feminine cries of alarm coming from the first-floor landing. *So much for the element of surprise,* he thought sourly.

Another gunblast came from below. Sam stayed down, and with good reason; Ellery was getting his range at last.

Suddenly the whole place was in pandemonium. Splinters flew from the balusters as the doorman's second bullet impacted barely eighteen inches from Sam's position. Doors were opening along the hallway above. Men's cries were mingling with the women's screams.

Rising, Sam leaned over the banister and took aim on the doorman below. Ellery had the Henry cocked and ready for his third shot, but seeing Sam's gun pointed his way, the doorman gave a yell, turned and disappeared like a short beer.

Suddenly growing aware that he was being

watched from above, Sam whirled back to face the head of the stairs. The breath caught in his throat as he came face to face with Baylor Ryan.

'*You!*' The red-head fairly spat the word. He was naked from the waist up, his right shoulder bandaged tightly.

Sam turned the Remington onto him. 'You're under arrest, Ryan! *All* of you are!'

But as laid-up as he was with his right hand, Ryan still held his Peacemaker in his left, and wasted no time in bringing it up to line. A gunblast roared. Sam ducked. When he came back up, the landing was empty.

He took the rest of the stairs two at a time. A dark-haired gent who appeared from the stairway above yelped at the sight of Sam's gun.

The man from Austin Springs was about half a second from blowing the near-naked fellow to perdition before he realised that he wasn't one of the boys he was after. 'Get back upstairs!' he snapped. 'And don't show your face again until all this is over!'

There was still plenty of noise coming from the first-floor hallway, but nobody was in sight when Sam peered around the corner. He was just about to begin his advance when a deep, authoritative woman's voice stopped him.

'You! Whoever you are, hold it!'

He turned to see a hennaed harridan covering him with a Colt's Lightning from the second-floor landing. She was big and she was brassy, and she was a fifty-year-old trying hard to be twenty. She wore a revealing powder-blue negligee and had her red hair up in curlers, but her face was already heavily made up, despite the early hour and the fact that, until Sam had come a-calling, she'd been fast asleep.

'I am Lily Clubb,' she said with some dignity as she came down two steps. 'I own this establishment. Now just who the hell are you?'

Before he could reply he caught a movement from the corner of his eye and ducked just as Raul Sadillo appeared from a door about thirty feet down the hall and blasted three shots at him from a blued .45.

Sam back-stepped hastily to get the corner between them, then came back, low, firing once, twice, again.

Raul screamed and flew backwards, discharging one more shot into the floor before collapsing. Behind Sam, Lily Clubb went very pale, screamed and fainted. She dropped the Lightning and fell – heavily, and with much wobbling – down the rest of the stairs to come to a halt at his feet.

Ignoring her, Sam dipped into his jacket pocket for fresh ammunition. With trembling fingers he spilled the spent cartridges from his gun and hurriedly reloaded.

Fifteen seconds passed, no more. The next time he appeared in the hallway entrance, however, it was to see Jim Dalton following Ryan and Hayes out a window and down the fire stairs at the rear of the building.

'*Damn!*'

Sam legged it along the hallway and quickly checked on Sadillo. The Mexican was bleeding from a bullet wound high in the chest, but Sam had seen such wounds before. Raul would probably live if a sawbones jammed something into the hole quick enough.

Leaving the bullet-struck Mexican to roll and groan, he turned and headed back the way he had come. He had no doubt that the fleeing outlaws would expect him to pursue them from above. By going back downstairs to catch them from below, he might regain the element of surprise.

Another gunshot brought him up short. *Damn – the doorman!*

Spinning, he brought the Remington up just as Ellery, who had reappeared in the doorway leading to the servants' quarters, brought his Henry up again.

Sam fired.

Ellery screamed and fell backwards, his right hand streaking up to his shattered left bicep. The repeater fell forgotten to the carpet as he tried to stem the tide of blood from his wound.

Now everything was a blur for the ageing

lawman. He leapt the last four stairs, bolted for the door, hauled it open, ran outside, turned right–

Another short dash brought him to the corner of the whorehouse. Cautiously he peered around it. Empty. Sucking in the dry, still air of early morning, he hot-footed it to the rear of the building, reaching it just in time to see Lester Hayes disappearing around the far side of the house.

'*Hell on a holiday!*' Sam roared.

Wheezing hard – for the air was still thin at this altitude – he made it along the back of the house and past the fire stairs in a kind of shambling trot. But before he could reach the corner around which Hayes had just vanished, he heard a noise coming from behind him. From behind – and *above*.

K-ching, k-ching, k-ching.

As he recognised the sound of Jim Dalton's spurs, he turned to see the sharp-eyed youngster still two flights up the fire stairs, peering down at him with murder on his face. Sam brought his gun around fast –

but too late. Dalton – his jaw still bruised from where Hayes had knocked him out a few nights before – already had his Dance Brothers .44 aimed and blasting.

Sam dived for the only cover available – three garbage pails – just as Dalton's two bullets struck the spot where he'd just been. The lawman landed awkwardly, harder than intended, knocked the wind out of his sails and saw stars.

K-ching, k-ching, k-ching!

The sonofabitch was hurrying now, desperate to get down the stairs and close in for the kill. Before he could make the last flight, however, a third figure appeared from the corner around which Sam had so recently come.

'Hold it, Jim!'

Sam screwed his eyes tight shut in an effort to refocus them. While they were closed he heard Dalton scream a furious oath and then a fusillade of small arms' fire. His vision returned just as Dalton jerked under the impact of two slugs, clawed at the blood ribboning from his chest, danced backwards, lost his balance – and fell over the guard-rail to land twenty feet below.

On his head.

The silence that followed the crunch was eerie. Until–

'Sam! Sam, you all right?'

Sam got to his feet just as the newcomer reached him at a run, his young, square-jawed face and gunmetal eyes showing his concern. At the sight of him, Sam could only register surprise.

'Matt!' he rasped, addressing his son. 'Just what in the name of Abraham Lincoln're *you* doin' here?'

Before Matt Dury could reply, a stern voice from the corner Sam had been heading for when Jim Dalton had attempted to back-shoot him barked, 'All right, you men! Stay right where you are!'

Still strung up taut from the recent action, Sam and his young companion turned to face this new threat with tight jaws and tighter guts. But then they allowed themselves to relax a little as an eight-strong deputation of townsmen approached them in a ragged line. They looked moody as hell, the lot of them, but not all that mean. Their average age was around the thirty-five mark. Some wore beards, some wore moustaches, some just settled for stubble. But all carried guns, mostly Winchester rifles, although they were held casually, not in any way that might provoke more shooting.

As a sign of good faith, Sam slipped his .44 back into leather. Following his lead, Matt returned his right-side Tranter to the two-gun *buscadero* rig buckled around his narrow hips.

'That's better,' growled the man at the head of the group. He was short and portly, dressed in grey duck pants, a somewhat creased clawhammer coat and a derby which sat atop his balding dome. He was older than the men behind him by maybe as many as fifteen years, with a smooth, clean-shaven face and jowls smudged crimson by a faint hint of blood pressure. He was wheeling a frail-looking imported Howe bicycle alongside him as if it were his most prized possession. When he wasn't heading up a vigilance committee, Sam figured he was more than likely a storekeeper.

'I am Herman Calhoun,' he went on with much self-esteem, 'the mayor of this fine town. Just who in blazes're you, and what is the meaning of all this commotion?'

There was no time for long-winded explanations, not now. Every second Sam and Matt were delayed meant a better chance of escape for Ryan and Hayes. So Sam took the initiative, remembering one very sound piece of advice imparted to him many years before: if in doubt, bull your way through.

Pulling aside the flap of his buckskin jacket to reveal his badge of office, he said, 'The name's Judge, Mr Mayor, town law for Austin Springs, Colorado. All this gunplay here was in the nature of official business. We're huntin' down a gang of robbers 'n' murderers, y'see.' Indicating Dalton's still form, he explained briskly, 'That's one of 'em there. You'll find another one bleedin' buckets up on the first floor of these here premises, so I'd be obliged if you could arrange for this 'un to be embalmed and stuck on ice and the other to receive some patchin' up and lockin' away pendin' my return.'

Mayor Calhoun looked completely dumb-founded. He might have been the local dignitary, but he didn't know squat about jurisdiction, warrants and the like, else he'd have come right out and told Sam he had no business being there at all. 'You mean … those other two fellows–'

'You saw 'em?' Sam demanded. 'Where were they heading?'

The mayor gestured vaguely north-east. 'That way, over towards Miss Lily's stables.'

'How far?'

''Bout a hundred yards,' Matt cut in. 'I passed it on the way here.'

Calhoun, meanwhile, was busy looking wretched. 'By rights I guess I should have sent a couple of men to apprehend them.'

'I reckon you did better *not* to,' Sam replied. 'These fellers're desperate, mayor. They got nothin' to lose. No matter what they do now, the law can only hang 'em the once.'

'Oh dear!'

Careful, so's not to spook the rest of the townsmen, the marshal reached into his pocket and brought out his billfold. 'I 'preciate your co-operation, Mr Mayor,' he said quickly. 'Mighty public-spirited of you, I don't mind sayin'. Here … fifteen dollars ought to be enough to pay for a doctor and a mortician, oughtn't it? Thanks.' He stuffed three fives into Calhoun's free hand, then glanced at his young sidekick. 'Come on, Deputy Dury – let's get after 'em!'

'But – but – see here, Judge! I can't just let you hightail it like this!' The balding mayor was trying hard to retain his authority. Indicating the whorehouse to illustrate his point, he said, 'I mean, there's still the question of damages to be settled!'

'Uh, that's right,' Sam replied, figuring that the best way to keep a man off balance was to agree with him all the time. 'You better tell the woman that owns the place, Chubb or Clubb or whatever her name is, that she'll have to contact the sheriff of Grover County, Colorado. He'll handle it. Now, if you don't mind...'

'Just a moment, marshal!'

Sam paused in mid-stride, trying hard to keep his temper in check. 'What now?' he asked.

Calhoun indicated his Howe. 'I, ah, I was wondering if you'd like the use of my 'cycle to go after these outlaws?'

Sam kept a poker face whilst looking at the contraption. 'Not hardly,' he replied. 'But thanks anyway.'

Then he and Matt were pushing through the line of men in front of them, intent on continuing their pursuit of the last of the Austin Springs bank robbers.

EIGHT

As they took the corner and began hustling cautiously around the shells of partially-constructed stores and offices toward the high-sided stable Lily Clubb provided for the convenience of her clients, Sam threw a glance at Matt's profile.

'You didn't answer my question,' he said.

Matt was reloading his Tranter on the move. 'You mean, what am I doing here?'

'That's the one,' Sam confirmed with a nod. 'Oh, don't get me wrong, boy. I'm grateful for your help 'n' all. Couldn't have been easy for you, shootin' a feller you used to ride with. But the last time I saw you, you was sleepin' like a baby in one of my lock-ups, tryin' to get over two busted ribs an' some serious bruisin'. What happened?'

'I healed,' the boy replied simply, returning Sam's sidelong glance. 'Healed an' got tired of sittin' around. Hell, you know what it's like.' Having finished replacing the handgun's spent shells, he slipped it back into leather. 'Anyway, I figured I'd try an' make myself useful, do somethin' to make up for … well, for what you did to square everythin' 'tween me an' the law.'

Certainly Matt looked better than he had the last time Sam had seen him. He walked straight-backed and tall again, the slim body beneath his striped Californian pants, plain cotton shirt and worn leather vest hinting at the return of his compact strength.

'Truth to tell,' he said as Sam ran a critical eye over him, 'I thought I'd get here too late, you havin' had a couple of weeks' start on me, but it looks like I made it just in time.'

'Well,' Sam replied, keeping his wary gaze on the land ahead now, 'I had a couple of distractions along the way.' Briefly, and in a low voice, he recounted the story of his run-in with Art Casey up around Long Branch, and the bout of 'flu that followed it. Wisely figuring it was about time he set a good example to the boy, he refrained from mentioning Amelia Brewer.

By now he could see the stable passably well through a man-made forest of stout wooden scaffolding. Which meant that they were just about as near as Sam wanted them to get for now. The place stood at about the centre of what would one day be a busy thoroughfare. To either side of it rose the skeletal forms of buildings still under construction, frameworks littered with mountains of timber and tiles that mirrored similar chaos on the opposite side of the street.

The two men went down low and crept nearer, finally hunkering down behind a pile of rough-cut lumber almost directly opposite their destination. Sam studied the place keenly, but nothing moved out on the empty street save the odd spiral of sand, blown east to west by a warm and gentle breeze.

Only one of the two 8 x 8 stable doors was still closed. The other one was open to reveal an interior full of shadows. No sound came from within, leastways nothing that Sam could detect. It crossed his mind that maybe Ryan and Hayes had already saddled up and lit out, but he didn't think it all that likely.

''Less'n I miss my guess,' he whispered to Matt, who was crouched beside him, 'this Ryan *hombre* doesn't know that you're involved in this yet. He thinks it's just me against him an' the other one.'

'Les.'

Something about the boy's wistful tone made Sam flash him a sharp look. Matt's dark eyes were fixed on the stable. He was absolutely motionless, and sweating harder than the still-early heat warranted. 'You all right, boy?' Sam asked, frowning.

Matt blinked, nodded. 'Sure.'

But there was a hollowness to his tone that worried the lawman. Softening his voice a little, he said, 'It's okay, boy, I know how you feel. There just ain't no easy way to go up agin fellers you called friends not so long back. Happen you'd feel better sittin' this one out–'

'No. No, Sam. I dealt myself in; I'll see it through.'

They locked stares. Sam recognised determination on the boy's face. 'All right. Now… You think you can get across the street without bein' spotted? I figure them looters'll try goin' out the back way as soon as I challenge 'em from the front. Be real nice if you could be there to greet 'em.'

Matt studied their surroundings closely, clamping his emotions down in an effort to become as dispassionate as he could. After a second or two he pointed off to their left and said, 'If I go far enough that way … a couple hundred feet should do it … that scaffoldin' an' lumber ought to cover me, no problem.'

'Okay. Soon as I see that you're in position then, I'll call on 'em to surrender. After that … well, after that, it'll be up to them.'

Matt nodded, looking very young.

'You be all right, son?'

'Sure.'

Sam swallowed. 'Go on then, an' keep low. An' Matt. If they *do* decide to make a fight of it...'

'Yeah?'

Sam drew his gun. 'Give 'em hell.'

For Baylor Ryan, the day had started with a muffled cry of warning from Lily Clubb's doorman.

Baylor had jerked awake, confused, his mind still sluggish. What was the old goat spouting about? A raid? A *raid?*

Then came the first of the gunfire.

The red-head had rolled out of bed then, and grabbed for his pants. Beside him, his top-heavy companion for the night sat up, her round, ringlet-framed face a picture of alarm. 'Oh my God! What's happening, Bay? What do you suppose–'

'*How the hell do I know?*'

He's snatched up his Peacemaker, wincing at the sudden stabbing pain in his still-sore shoulder, and cursed. Then he tore open the bedroom door, stepped out into the hallway. The gunfire had sounded more like thunder out there, closer, sharper, deadlier. What was going on? He couldn't even guess. Cautiously, he made it to the head of the stairs, and saw–

'*You!*'

The man from Austin Springs was just about the last person he'd expected to find here; as soon as Baylor clapped eyes on him he felt a surge of fear shoot through him.

But it didn't take him long to recover, nor to realise that the lawman was here to arrest him.

Anyplace else, the idea might have been laughable. But how many men had Judge brought with him? Was the place surrounded? Baylor didn't know and couldn't guess. And without knowing the odds–

He spooked. Bad.

Almost without thinking about it, he brought up the Colt in his fist and fired a wild, covering shot. Then he turned, racing back to his room, a thin wisp of smoke trailing from his gun barrel.

Somehow Hayes materialised before him. Like Baylor, he had donned his pants, shrugged into a dull grey shirt too. For one split second Baylor saw fear on his wide, ebony face; then Les got it under control, or just about.

'What is it, Bay? Bay, what's happ'nin'?'

Baylor pushed past him, dashed back into his room, grabbed his boots, his shirt, weapons-belt, the burlap sack that still contained most of his share of the robbery money. Hayes followed him like a lost sheep. Still in bed, the whore watched them both through scared eyes.

'Bay?'

Before the red-head could answer her, they heard a man's startled yelp, then Sam's voice carrying to them from down the hall. *'Get back upstairs – and don't show your face again until all this is over!'*

Swallowing, Hayes said, 'Who ... who *is* it? Who's that out there?'

Ryan turned back to him, his face hot and

flushed, his blue eyes wide and bulging. '*Judge!*' he snarled.

Hayes frowned. 'Judge?'

'*Sam* Judge! Matt's friend, the lawman!'

Uncharacteristically, the black boy swore. 'Holy Mother'a God, what's *he* doin' here?'

'What do you think? Now get outta my way, Les! Get your gear together. We gotta get out of here!'

And they had. Somehow.

But Raul and Jim ... they hadn't been so lucky. Baylor had seen Judge shoot Raul, seen Raul go down, bleeding bad. Chances were that the little Mex was dead by now.

As for Jim ... well, he didn't know for sure, of course, but ... but he'd heard the volley of gunshots that came from behind the joy-house as he and Les had legged it for the stable and their horses. It was easy enough to fill in the details when Jim never showed up to join them.

At last their twisting, turning flight through the confusion of partly-erected buildings brought them to Miss Lily's stable. They burst out onto the empty street and crossed it at a staggering run. As they threw themselves through the open door they were gasping like old-timers themselves. But now anger was replacing panic, at least as far as Baylor was concerned. He was being torn between the desire to run and the need to get even.

As they waited for their breath to return, the red-head took a quick look around the stable. It was approximately fifty feet square and stank of dung. Along the north wall stood ten stalls, most of them occupied. Opposite had been parked a rickety-looking buckboard. At the rear of the place lay a selection of saddles and associated gear. In the back wall another set of high doors opened out onto a corral.

Staying just inside the front entrance, Baylor told Les to get their horses saddled up fast while he kept an eye on their back-trail.

'Ah *knowed* we should'a listened to Matt,' the black boy lamented as he crossed over to the pile of saddles to do as instructed. 'He warned us not to go agin that Judge feller.

Reckon we should'a heeded him!'

Baylor ignored him, squinting out across the empty street and beyond, trying to find some sign of their pursuer through the frameworks standing along the other side of the street.

'...come on, if you're comin'...' he whispered impatiently.

Les called his name softly. 'Iffen you come an' give me a hand, we' get this done twice as quick!'

Anxiety had given his stentorian voice a petulant air that irritated hell out of Baylor. 'Forget it,' the red-head growled without looking around. 'Do it yourself, Les – on the double, too. I ain't takin' my eyes offa this here street.'

With jittery fingers and a choice selection of cuss-words, Hayes completed preparing the first horse, his own bay gelding, for their getaway. Leaving the animal ground-hitched at the rear of the building, he started back to the pile of saddles to fetch Baylor's rig.

And that was then they heard it.

'Ryan! Hayes! This here's Sam Judge from Austin Springs! You know why I'm here! Now throw out your weapons an' get on out here with your hands up!'

As one minute stretched into another, Sam had started worrying about his son. What the hell was keeping him? Was it possible that something had happened to him?

Then a faint movement about thirty yards along the other side of the street caught his eye. Turning his head that way, he felt a rush of relief as he saw Matt picking a cautious path towards the back of the stable, crouch-walking with both guns drawn.

As soon as the boy was lost to sight again, Sam counted off a slow thirty seconds until he estimated that Matt was in position. Then he drew in a deep breath and yelled his challenge.

Almost immediately a figure just inside the doorway – most likely Ryan – loosed off a couple of wild shots. Sam ducked instinctively, although with the thick pile of lumber between him and the stable, there was no real need.

Coming around his makeshift cover, he returned fire twice, just to let them know he meant business. His slugs hit the stable's weathered planks in an explosion of dust and splinters. After a moment, Ryan fired again.

'Listen up in there!' Sam bellowed. 'I'm tryin' to give you a chance to surrender peaceably! Take it an' I promise you a fair trial!'

'Go to hell!'

Sam ducked again as more angry slugs slapped into the other side of the lumber pile, spraying yellow needles of Sitka spruce high into the air.

'Come on, Baylor, Ah finished here!'

Ryan tossed a darting glance over his shoulder. Hayes was holding both horses by their bridles, fighting hard to keep them from pulling loose and bolting at the exchange of gunfire.

'Well I ain't finished *here*,' the red-head rasped.

'Huh?'

Ryan had already returned his gaze to the framework directly opposite the stable, and more specifically the pile of rough-cut timber lying back in the patchy shadows about a hundred feet away. 'I already run once today,' he said in a strangely calm tone. 'Don't figure to do it again.'

'What you talkin' 'bout, Bay?'

'That sonofabitch Judge is what I'm talkin' about!' Ryan replied, punctuating his words with gunfire. 'What happens if we run? Huh? He'll only come after us. Better we settle his hash now, once an' for all!'

Return fire from Sam's position made the horses pull and stamp more, not just the two in Hayes' grip, but all of them. Fear was a palpable thing in the shadow-filled livery, a demon that haunted man and beast alike.

'Don't be a fool!' cried the Negro. 'We don't even know how many men that badge-packer's got with him! Might be fifteen, twenty, might be more! Better to cut 'n' run, try an' lose ourselves, maybe Mexico or someplace, or hole up an' choose the time 'n' place for a showdown that suits *us*–'

'Les,' barked Ryan. 'If you wanna run, you go right ahead an' do it.'

'Damn you, Bay, I ain't no coward!'

'Then stop actin' like one an' get your black ass over here to give me some help!'

Hayes found himself in an agony of indecision. He just didn't know which way to jump for the best. He was long on loyalty and would back his friends to the hilt. But this time surely it was better to run. After all, how could a man fight an enemy he didn't even know the size of?

In any event, his decision was made for him by a quiet, authoritative voice that came from behind.

'Don't move a muscle, Les. You're under arrest. You too, Bay.'

There was a moment of complete surprise as the bank robbers recognised the voice of their captor. Wheeling around, they found

Matt standing in the corral doorway, covering them with both Tranters held steady.

'*Matt!*'

Hayes' reaction was something akin to relief. Baylor's, on the other hand, was exactly the opposite.

His fury finally boiling over and his sweat-streaked face screwing into a map of hate, he yelled something unintelligible and let loose with the Peacemaker until it was clicking on empty.

Doing the only thing he could in the circumstances, Matt went down flat on his belly while Ryan's slugs chewed up the woodwork around the corral doors.

For a dozen heartbeats nothing existed but the endless crash of gun-thunder. Then silence poured over the scene and Matt came up into a crouch, right-side Tranter extended. But still he held back from firing, not through any last-minute feelings of kinship but simply because the two saddle-horses were snorting and side-stepping, making it difficult for him to draw a clear enough bead on his target.

'Dammit!'

Suddenly he heard a noise. A snarl. Baylor. *'Give me that!'* The bay gelding hopped to one side just as Baylor pistol-whipped Hayes, opening a deep slice down his face, and dragging the Negro's Navy .36 from leather.

As Hayes collapsed groaning, Matt took aim again and yelled. 'Hold it, Bay – or I fire!'

'Damn you, you turncoat bastard!'

Another reckless shot; Matt ducked low. When he came up again, Lester Hayes was already back on his knees with his hands raised high, blood streaming down his ashen face, the horses still prancing skittishly around him. 'All right, Matt, all right, jus' don't shoot!'

Matt rose to his full height, ignoring him, his attention fixed only on Baylor now.

But Baylor was no longer in the stable with them.

With a cry more animal than human, Baylor burst out into the dusty sunlight with the heavy Navy .36 cocked and ready for mayhem.

As soon as Sam saw him, all thought for Matt's safety was pushed to the back of his mind. No matter what had happened, or what was *about* to happen, this was to be the final confrontation, he felt sure. Powering up out of his crouch, he leapt over the pile of lumber and raised his Remington for a warning shot.

The blast cut through Baylor's blue funk and brought him up sharp. Coming back to his senses, he swung to face Sam just as the marshal yelled, 'That's far enough, Ryan! Drop that gun and grab some sky!'

Baylor did no such thing.

With another defiant roar he began firing non-stop at the lawman. Sam dodged to one side as lead whistled around him, fired back, missed. Then something hot and invisible punched him in the right shoulder and he staggered. The little voice in his mind was tinged with disbelief as he thought, *I'm shot. The sonuver actually shot me.*

With a cry more of anger than pain, Sam collapsed in the dirt.

As he lay squirming on the ground, Baylor's blue eyes lit up with an almost obscene triumph. With infinite care – or so it seemed through Sam's pain-racked vision – the bank robber prepared to deliver his killing shot. Sam could almost see his finger whitening around the handgun's trigger.

But then the two saddle-horses, taking advantage of their freedom now that Lester Hayes was no longer in any position to hold them back, erupted through the stable doorway to collide with the red-head.

The impact was harrowing just to watch. As Baylor was smashed to the ground with bone-snapping force, the gun left his hand. He sprawled on his stomach trying desperately to curl up into a ball. For a moment he was lost behind a screen of dust as the horses pounded over him and hightailed it up the street, eventually stumbling on their trailing reins.

Then the dust settled back over his pitiful form.

'…help … me … help me, damn you…!'

Matt appeared in the stable doorway, looking down at his one-time friend with shock carved into his bloodless face. Lester Hayes joined him a moment later, a kerchief held up to his gun-gashed cheek.

Then Matt tore his eyes away from the broken figure in the sand to seek out that of his adopted 'uncle'. 'Sam! You–'

'Yeah,' Sam called back tiredly. 'I'm fine. Or leastways I will be when I get a sawbones to take a look at this here arm o' mine. You got a horse nearby?'

Matt nodded, a tentative smile shooing some of the seriousness from his long, lightly weathered face. 'Kind of,' he replied. 'Nothin' special, but a sturdy enough little cow-pony. I talked your friend Meares into lettin' me buy her on credit.'

'Well, you better go an' fetch her,' Sam advised, climbing slowly to his feet and inspecting his blood-stained shoulder. 'From the looks of him, I'd say we better get Red here to a doctor pretty fast–'

'Right!'

'–iffen he's gonna live long enough to hang,' Sam finished quietly.

Austin Springs, Colorado; twelve days and a hundred miles later.

It was sometime around mid-morning when word went out that the marshal was riding back into town with his prisoners in tow. After that, news travelled fast, fed by a sense of excitement and anticipation. Men told women; wives told husbands; curious children, overhearing the news, promptly told their friends.

One by one they all came out from their homes and stores and offices to watch the short, silent procession pass them by on the way to Sam's First Street office: Heck Mabey, the butcher, Katy Larrimer, Len Meares, Wallace Corey, Doc Hobson's widow, the grieving parents of little Vicky

Trotter – and Nell Redmond, holding her two-week-old baby boy, whom she had named John after her late husband.

Wagons came to a halt at the spectacle. Riders reined in to stare. It was as if the whole town had come to a standstill, which, in fact, it had.

Sam rode at the head of the small column, slump-shouldered and worn out, his only thoughts now of a bath and a change of clothes and later, a good night's sleep on a decent feather mattress. His right arm was still rigid, and prone to the most nagging of aches, but the Linarez doctor who'd operated to remove Baylor's bullet had told him to take that as a sign of healing.

Behind the marshal came a rattling tumbleweed wagon, in effect a cell on wheels, which Matt was driving. They'd borrowed the contraption from George Murphy up in Long Branch to make the return trip as easy on themselves and their prisoners as they could.

As they came to the familiar solidly-built adobe square of Sam's office, Matt hauled back on the reins of the team animals Murphy had released into their care and stepped on the brake, bringing the dust-covered wagon to a slow and shuddering halt.

Sam climbed down from his roan and tied the horse to the hitch-rack outside the building. Then he lifted Mitzi down from her saddle-bag and turned to his son, indicating the sturdy wood and iron-strapped compartment which had been built into the wagon's bed.

'Get 'em out of their an' herd 'em inside.'

'Yo!'

While Matt tied the ribbons around the brake and hopped easily down to the ground, Sam went up onto the porch. A sign on the law office door said: CLOSED UNTIL FURTHER NOTICE. ALL ENQUIRIES TO J. O'NEAL c/o AUSTIN SPRINGS HERALD. Not bothering to take the sign down, Sam tried the door handle. The door was unlocked, the office empty. Trudging through to the cell-block, he pulled a key-ring off the nail inside the doorway and unlocked the cubicles in readiness for their new occupants.

After a while they all shuffled through: Ryan, pale-faced and broken, still using crutches to take the strain off his fractured-but-mending left leg; Lester Hayes, walking head up in a desperate attempt to regain some of his lost dignity; Raul Sadillo, shambling and still breathless from the operation to remove Sam's bullet from his upper chest; and Art Casey, whom they had collected from Long Branch on their way back down from the high country.

Only one of the robbers was missing; after the Linarez county coroner had taken a look at him and signed the death certificate, Jim Dalton had been buried in the local cemetery.

Sam had just finished locking them all up when Jack O'Neal came through the door. The mayor looked as sophisticated as ever in a smart grey business suit, his snow-white hair combed back from his smooth, tanned face.

'Sam! My God, so it's true! You're actually back!'

The two men shook hands, Sam using his left out of necessity, while Matt busied himself starting a fire in the range in the corner.

'Tell me, then,' the mayor said enthusiastically. 'You got them, did you?' Almost absently he reached into his Prince Albert and passed Sam a hand-rolled Havana in a thin cardboard tube.

'That I did,' Sam replied. 'With a little help from Matt here. Any problems while I was gone?'

'Nope.'

'I didn't think there would be.'

'Well, not unless you count the holy Ned Dan Fetterman raised when he found out you'd gone off to take the law into your own hands,' O'Neal said as an afterthought, referring to the county sheriff.

'Oh, I expected that,' Sam allowed. 'Still, no problem. I'll make sure I appear fittin'ly sheepish when I see him.'

'See him?'

'Yeah.' The marshal pulled the cigar from its wrapper, bit off the end and struck a match along the side of his desk. 'I'm takin' these here prisoners in to the county seat in the mornin'. Shouldn't take more'n a couple'a days. Figure to hand 'em over to Fetterman pendin' their trial.' He looked up then, and there was something in his face and tone that made O'Neal know what he was going to add even before he said it. 'I won't be comin' back, Jack.'

'*What?*'

It was Matt who spoke, for this was as much news to him as it was to the mayor. He came over to stand beside O'Neal while Sam elaborated on his reasons for leaving, the shock and dismay on his face hard to hide.

'See,' Sam said around the cigar, 'on the way back here I finally got a chance to read the letter that came for me the day of the robbery. It was from an old friend of mine, a right fine lady I knew back in my Barbary Coast days.

'Anyway, to cut it down to basics, she married up with a star-packer over to Nevada way, little gold 'n' silver town called King Creek. Seems they been havin' some problems out there with a faction that's kind of set on takin' over the town an' runnin' things *their* way – which is plenty rough.'

'She's asked you to go out there and lend a hand,' guessed O'Neal.

Sam nodded. 'I'm sorry to spring it on you, Jack. If I could, I'd hang on an' work notice. But this lady I jus' now told you about, she sounds awful desperate.'

The mayor was thinking ahead now, to what must be done to elect a new peace-keeper for the community. 'Eh? Oh, yes, of course. You ... you've got to do whatever you think best, Sam. After all, we're settled here in Austin Springs. It's a town where nothing ever happens. Well, *hardly* ever.' His smile was sad. 'Still, it's going to be a heck of a shame to lose you, buddy.'

Matt watched the two men shake hands.

'Now,' said O'Neal, sentiment finished

and all business again. 'You'll have to excuse me. Things to do.'

'Sure.'

Once he'd gone, Sam put his feet up on the desk and made the most of his cigar. After a while Mitzi wandered in and leapt up onto his lap. Matt brought over a mug of coffee. 'Here,' he said, not looking Sam in the face. 'Black an' sweet, just how you like it, right?'

'Thanks. You not havin' one?'

Matt shook his head and reached for his hat. 'No … I … I gotta go make arrangements down at the livery to get Murphy's rig back to him. See to ol' Charlie and my pony, too, while I'm at it.'

'All right,' Sam replied. 'But don't be long. We got a lot to do afore we quit this burg in the mornin'.'

Almost imperceptibly the boy's long face brightened. 'We?'

Sam looked up at him and winked. 'Well, I figure I'm gonna need me some help when I reach King Creek,' he explained. 'I was kinda hopin' you'd want to tag along – as my deputy.'

'Well – uh – sure. If–'

'Good,' Sam smiled. 'That's settled, then.'

After the boy had gone, Sam sipped his coffee and threw a thoughtful glance at the closed door leading into the cell-block. It was such a waste, he thought sourly. Such a waste that four once-healthy boys would never get to grow up into men.

The hangman would see to that.

But Matt, so like them in some ways and yet so different in others ... he was destined for something else, something *better*. Sam felt certain of it.

Thinking of the challenges that lay ahead for them, he also felt a keen sense of anticipation. After all, they made a good team. Sam had wisdom – of a sort – that he wanted to pass on. And Matt was sensible enough to realise the value of learning it. No matter what awaited them in King Creek, Nevada, they would handle it the best way they could.

A good team, yeah.
Spring and autumn.
Father and son.
Judge and Dury.

The publishers hope that this book has given you enjoyable reading. Large Print Books are especially designed to be as easy to see and hold as possible. If you wish a complete list of our books please ask at your local library or write directly to:

Dales Large Print Books
Magna House, Long Preston,
Skipton, North Yorkshire.
BD23 4ND

This Large Print Book, for people
who cannot read normal print,
is published under the auspices of
THE ULVERSCROFT FOUNDATION